Double damn.

His head told him she would only leave again, but his gut warned him to slow down and think things through. If they'd made a child together, that baby was the only real family he had. And if Marissa took off out west somewhere, he might never find her. No way would he let that happen. Not until he'd found out the truth.

"All right, Marissa. You're on."

She whipped around to face him, her eyes wide and locked on his.

Good.

He might have to swallow his pride, accept her demands until things straightened themselves out. But that didn't mean he had to follow all the rules.

He crossed the room and stepped in front of her.

"I'll make concessions, just the way you asked. If it's courting you want, that's what you'll get."

Keeping his touch easy, he cupped his hand under her chin.

"Let's seal the deal."

Dear Reader,

Thanks for joining me in my publishing adventure and taking a look at this, my second Harlequin American Romance novel! I'm especially thrilled to have a book out right now, as it's one of my favorite times of the year.

No matter what holidays we celebrate, we're approaching a festive season. And I have a sneaking suspicion you might be like me, always excited at seeing a small wrapped box that could contain a new book—or three.

The novel you're holding now, as with many ideas, started with a what if: What if two people married, only to separate almost immediately...then discover they'd conceived a child? That idea—and the image of a man holding a wedding ring he can't force himself to throw away—gave me the basis for Gabe and Marissa's story. They'd given up on love, but I *had* to bring them together again. With a baby on the way, they had a lot to talk about....

I hope you enjoy reading this book as much as I enjoyed writing it. Feel free to drop me a note and let me know! You can reach me at P.O. Box 504 Gilbert, AZ 85299 or through my Web site, www.barbarawhitedaille.com.

All my best to you during the holiday season!

Until we meet again,

Barbara White Daille

Court Me, Cowboy
BARBARA WHITE DAILLE

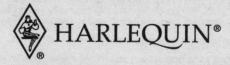

TORONTO • NEW YORK • LONDON
AMSTERDAM • PARIS • SYDNEY • HAMBURG
STOCKHOLM • ATHENS • TOKYO • MILAN • MADRID
PRAGUE • WARSAW • BUDAPEST • AUCKLAND

ISBN-13: 978-0-373-75144-0
ISBN-10:   0-373-75144-3

COURT ME, COWBOY

This edition published by arrangement with Harlequin Books S.A.

® and TM are trademarks of the publisher. Trademarks indicated with ® are registered in the United States Patent and Trademark Office, the Canadian Trade Marks Office and in other countries.

www.eHarlequin.com

Printed in U.S.A.

ABOUT THE AUTHOR

When she was very young, Barbara White Daille learned from her mom about the storytelling magic in books—and she's been hooked ever since. Now thrilled to be an author herself, she hopes you will enjoy reading her books and will find your own magic in them! Originally from the East Coast, Barbara lives with her husband in the warm, sunny Southwest, where they love the dry heat and have taken up square dancing.

To inspirational author Marta Perry
for being a true inspiration and friend,
and to Rich for being my hero

~~~~~

Many thanks to Paula Eykelhof
for her graciousness...and her great memory

Chapter One

One day soon, he'd get rid of this wedding ring.

Gabe Miller tossed the gold circle into the air and snatched it back again, trying not to think of the woman who'd slipped it onto his left hand, third finger. Trying not to think of what she'd had inscribed inside.

Forever, M

What a crock. Forever hadn't lasted but three short weeks.

Scowling, he shoved the band into the velvet-lined jeweler's box and slid it back in place beneath the stack of flannel shirts in the dresser drawer. Call him a dumb cowboy, but it'd taken his own wife's desertion to finally get the familiar message rammed into his thick skull:

Never trust a woman.

"Yo, boss."

He turned. Warren stood in the bedroom doorway, his whiskered face scrunched into a frown.

"Shake a leg. The boys'll be raring to eat any minute now."

"Right." As Gabe headed down the hall in the wake of his elderly ranch hand, he cursed, then felt immediate guilt. Warren hadn't caused his ugly mood.

Their two pairs of boots sounded loud on the bare wooden stairs that led them to the first floor, where they entered the kitchen.

"We gotta get us a cook, boss. It's been nearly a month since Joe and Mary went back East." Warren flipped a switch, powering up the coffeemaker Gabe had gotten ready the night before. "Lord knows, a rancher's got enough to keep him moving sunup to sundown. And you're kept busier than most, managing this big spread yourself 'n all."

"We're doing just fine, Warren." He was careful to keep his tone neutral, knowing how much it grated on the older man that he couldn't pull his weight with the younger hands anymore.

"Yeah, long as you don't try gettin' too fancy."

"Okay, so the pancakes didn't work out so well."

That earned him a chuckle.

Gabe grabbed the egg carton and a pack of pork links from the refrigerator. Sure, having to undertake kitchen duties once his ranch cook and her husband had moved on had been the last thing he'd needed. Gabe *did* have more to handle than most of the local ranchers. Something Marissa hadn't understood.

He rubbed the back of his neck and swallowed a growl. He had to stop thinking of Marissa.

Lost cause, that idea. He brooded on it anyway. Why the heck had he woken up this morning—alone in his big bed—with the feeling today would turn out worse than the usual? He couldn't manage to push the gloom from his mind the way he'd shoved the wedding ring back under his flannel shirts. The ring he should have tossed out, just as she'd tossed him aside months ago.

That, right there, was the problem.

She'd walked out three months ago today.

Jared and Hank and the rest of the cowhands trooped into the kitchen. Their usual banter drowned out the sizzle of eggs and sausages.

"Hey, boys, hold it down a bit," Warren grumbled. "Don't know where you get your energy this early in the morning."

Gabe grimaced, knowing his own bad mood had caused the complaints. He was used to rowdy cowboys before the sun was even up—he'd breakfasted with ranch hands all his life. But he remembered best those days—those way too few days—when he'd skipped the chowdowns out at the bunkhouse to spend every last early-morning moment he could bedded down with his wife.

Hank, best known as the ranch's clown, looked over Gabe's shoulder. "No pancakes today, boss?"

The rest of the men guffawed.

"All right, so I'm not much of a cook." *Marissa was.* He shook the thought away. "Better knock it off, or y'all will be taking turns at the stove."

Silence fell heavier than a bale dropped from the hayloft. His back still turned to his men, he reached for the egg carton again and grinned. Shut *them* up, all right.

In the calm, he heard the noise of a car's engine. Awfully early for visitors.

Warren pushed up the blind over the kitchen sink and squinted through the window. "Seems like you got company, boss." The old cowboy's voice had gone rusty.

Gabe stepped to his side. "Must be Doc. Nobody else'd—"

What he saw, though, shut *him* up, too. The light over the back porch stabbing through predawn darkness. The white Mustang purring in the drive. And the woman sitting behind the wheel.

Marissa.

He must still be sleeping after all, must be dreaming. But blinking didn't help. The image remained. He closed his eyes for a long moment and opened them again. Nope, she was still there.

Looking right at the lighted kitchen window. Right at him.

He stumbled back a pace.

"Easy, now." Warren might have been talking to a skittish colt. He pulled the forgotten carton of eggs from Gabe's hands. "Got it under control here, boss. I guess you got some business needs taking care of."

"Yeah, right." He glanced through the window again, gritted his teeth and set his jaw.

He had something to take care of, all right.

Throwing his ex-wife off his land.

Flexing his suddenly unsteady fingers, he crossed the

kitchen to yank open the wooden back door. His heavy breath hit the cold morning air, spewing white mist in front of him like some smoke-and-fire-breathing dragon.

Feeling afire himself, he strode along the porch, down the steps and across the wide expanse of dirt between the house and the driveway, powered by three months of misery and—worse—the poorly disguised pity of his men, his neighbors, his friends.

Seduced by a pretty face. Shamed by one, too, going from like to love in thirty-five seconds, with a quick detour for lust in between.

He should've stopped at that bend.

Then again, he should've known better than to hook up with her at all. He wasn't the kind of man who was good at loving a woman. Or having a woman love him. He'd lived with that knowledge for most of his life.

Marissa had made him forget it. For a very short time.

He moved down the driveway toward the Mustang, an easy target in the light streaming from the porch.

His anger raged…but sanity ruled.

As he neared the car, he began to slow, struggling to calm himself, to uncurl his fingers, to take a deep breath. Memories of Marissa, their brief marriage, and her curt rejection had him riled.

But tough Texas cowboys didn't let emotions overtake them.

By the time he reached the Mustang, he managed to set his hands lightly on the frame above the open driver's window and crook his mouth up on one side.

"You needing directions somewhere?" *Good.* Lazy smile. Laid-back tone. Peaceable question. He'd done himself proud.

She couldn't seem to say a word. His body blocked the light from her face, making those huge hazel eyes he remembered so well look blue-black in the shadows.

Her lips parted a bit. Before he could stop himself, his gaze shot to her full, rosy mouth. It had been a long time since he'd had it under his.

That wasn't something he should be thinking.

In the dead silence, a horse neighed, maybe in warning.

Seeing her reach for the door handle, he backed up a few feet and crossed his arms over his chest.

She climbed from the car and stood in front of him, a petite bundle of woman barely reaching his chin. Her body looked shapeless beneath her bulky jacket. Didn't matter. His traitorous memory called to mind every feminine curve and hollow.

His mouth felt filled with prairie dust.

The harsh porch lighting washed out her delicate features and peachy complexion, but it couldn't hide her high cheekbones and firm chin. Couldn't fade the fawn-colored hair tumbling in waves around her shoulders. Those heavy strands had spilled around his shoulders, too, when she'd rested against his chest after they'd made love….

The thought toughened his resolve. She'd staked a claim on him once, then abandoned it. "What do you want, Marissa?"

"We need to talk."

"Nothing to talk about." Three months of misery. The thought drove him forward. "You're nothing to me anymore."

"I'm your wife."

"The hell you are. You left a note saying you'd have the marriage ended. Get it annulled. I sent you the papers, registered."

"I know you did. But I didn't."

"You're not making sense."

"And you're making me nervous." Worry lines creased her forehead. She clenched her hands in front of her, her fingers twisting like old rope.

Not thinking, he uncrossed his arms to reach out to her, then caught himself. What the hell was he doing? More important, what the hell was she trying to pull? He shouldn't have trusted her back then; he sure wouldn't trust her now. Clinging to what he knew, instead of reaching for what he had loved and lost, he nearly spit, "We're divorced."

"We're not. I'm sorry, Gabe. This isn't the way I'd planned to tell you. But the truth is, I never filed the paperwork. We're still married."

He shook his head to clear it. This conversation had doubled back faster than his best cow dog at roundup. "So I'll take care of the paperwork myself. No problem. You can just hop on back in your car and head out."

"It's not that easy."

"What do you mean?" His gut churned.

She looked toward the house. "Do you think we could go inside, where we could have a little privacy?"

"You want to be alone with me?"

Her gaze shot to his, then darted away.

"We're fine right here." He didn't want her setting foot in his house again. Didn't want her this close to him, even. He crossed his arms over his chest once more, readying himself for the next blow.

After a while, her eyes crept back to meet his. "This isn't the way I'd planned to tell you this, either, but…"

His mind raced with scenarios, trying to figure out what more she could have done.

"What are you afraid of, Marissa? Nothing beats running out on me." He laughed, low and without humor, and added in a mocking tone, "What happened? You maxed out the credit card I gave you? Defaulted on a loan? Got arrested and used my name to make bail? It's all right. Whatever it is, I'll deal with it."

What was it?

The skin between his shoulder blades prickled, reminding him of the nearness of the kitchen window. He should have kept setting breakfast up in the bunkhouse kitchen, instead of bringing the boys to the main house. Then again, they'd provided him with a built-in excuse for not taking Marissa inside.

"I've got a ranch to run," he reminded her, "so why don't you say your piece and be on your way?"

Her deep breath sent a plume of white toward him. Her gaze skittered somewhere out past the barn. And her voice broke as she whispered words he had to bend closer to catch.

"We're having a baby."

WHAT A MESS she had gotten herself into.

Marissa eased into the kitchen. Gabe followed at her heels, closing the heavy door with a bang.

The men who sat around the long wooden trestle table jumped to their feet, chair legs screeching against linoleum, nearly drowning out their mumbled "Mornings" and "Ma'ams." They bobbed their heads and stared at her.

After giving them a brittle smile, she sank into the nearest vacant seat. The cowboys backed away as if she had some dreaded disease.

She glanced down at the table, then shuddered. The breakfast dishes, wiped clean, did her chef's heart good. But the plate at the other end of the table nearly did her in. The remains of sunny-side up eggs, runny yolk now congealing around a slice of cold toast, set off the queasiness she'd fought every morning for weeks.

Swallowing hard, she looked away.

The men had shifted their attention to Gabe. Reluctantly, she let hers wander there, as well.

She hadn't wanted to come here today. But her conscience had told her she must. She had to tell Gabe, face-to-face, about the baby. She wanted him aware, involved from the start. But she hadn't expected the sight of him to hit her so hard.

Her hands shook as she drank in the sight of the man she had never stopped wanting in all the months she'd been gone. The man she had conceived a child with—as far as she could determine—the very first time they'd made love.

She had loved him then, or so she'd thought.

For the first time in her life, she had been with someone who listened to her and made her feel important. He had made her feel loved and cherished and wanted.

She'd never been loved by anyone before.

And, yet, she'd never been more wrong.

He had carried her over the threshold, bringing her into this house that had never been her home. Then he'd left her to her own devices, while he spent seemingly his every waking moment at work on the ranch. The abruptness of the change had stunned her. Worse, it had turned Gabe into someone she didn't know at all.

Now, he stood in the middle of the kitchen, focused on his men. Bands of early-morning light filtered through the slatted wooden blinds, streaking his brown hair and making his light-brown eyes shine.

His voice rumbled through the crowded room as he told the cowboys to get started on the day's chores without him. The men nodded farewell to her, plucked their hats from the rack by the door and left the room at a near run.

Only Gabe remained.

He turned to her, and her throat tightened.

He grabbed a kitchen chair, flipped it around and straddled it, resting his arms on its back only inches from her.

She shifted, forcing a laugh. "Well, that was a first. At least, in my experience. In the two weeks I lived here, you never let the cowboys go off without you."

"I own the ranch. I work it."

"Work…" she repeated. "My point exactly. Work was your top priority." Her heart ached at the thought.

"Had to be. I've got bills owing, men who need paying. And, back then, I had a wife I needed to support." He shoved a breakfast plate aside, as if pushing his last comment away. Pushing *her* away. "Did you drive all night?"

"I stopped at a motel just a couple of hours away. I knew I would have to arrive before dawn to see you before you left the house for the day." She put a hand to her stomach, still taut and flat, showing no evidence at all of the life that grew within her.

"You're how far along?" he asked.

"About three and a half months."

He nodded and kept eyeing her. "And you're just getting around to telling me?"

"I didn't know myself until a couple of weeks ago."

His snort of derision radiated his disbelief. A chill ran through her. This wasn't going at all the way she had planned.

"It's true. I've always been irregular, so for the first couple of months I didn't even notice. But a few weeks ago, I started to wonder. A home-test kit confirmed what I suspected." She took a deep breath. "Gabe, you know there had to be a possibility of this happening."

He raised a brow.

"No," she whispered, barely able to breathe. "You don't believe me."

"Never said so."

"You didn't have to." Fighting a wave of nausea, she planted her arms on the table.

He shook his head. "Guess I'll just have to take your word for it."

"Which is exactly what you're *not* doing now. How could you, Gabe? How could you think I would ever—" She gave up. No sense wasting her breath. She gathered up her coat and stood. "I'm sorry I bothered you."

She'd almost made it to the back door when his voice stopped her.

"Running away again, Marissa?"

Chapter Two

Marissa froze, facing the door, as Gabe's taunting voice continued behind her.

"Aren't you headed the wrong way? You've just told me I'm gonna be a daddy. With something like that to celebrate, you ought to be throwing yourself into my arms."

She gave a strangled laugh and had to close her eyes against the thought of being held close to him again. His kisses, his caresses had been her downfall once, but never again. "I don't think so. In your arms is the last place I should be."

"Honey, that's no way to act, now that we're going to be a family."

A *family*. Her heart lurched at the word, at the dream she'd long held and never realized. Never would.

But what about the baby?

That was all that mattered. She had to think of their child.

She turned around. "Gabe, clearly, our marriage

was a mistake. I decided it was best to walk away from it." *From you.*

A muscle ticked in his jaw. "So what brought you back here?"

"I had to tell you about the baby, of course."

Again, he made a derisive sound. "Not good enough, Marissa. You could have called. Sent a telegram. A letter."

"You're right. I could have done any of those things." She paused, trying to dredge up the speech she had prepared and rehearsed and memorized on the long drive from Chicago. "But I felt you had the right to hear it from me directly."

"So you just decided to hop in the car and drive nine hundred miles to give me the news."

"Yes. I was leaving Chicago, anyway."

"What, you just up and quit that big-city job of yours?"

She answered his mocking question with a forced, measured reply. "Yes, I quit my job. They'll get along without me. And, for your information, I gave two weeks' notice first."

Conveniently, her leaving had coincided with Father's month-long business trip to Europe. The news would take a while to rise through the chain of command to his lofty level. Add one more item to the list of things he didn't yet know about his daughter. Such as her pregnancy. And her marriage.

Clearing her throat, she continued, "I'm heading out West, not sure where yet. I'll let you know. I'll file the paperwork for the divorce, but of course you'll want visiting rights. I'll be in touch later about making those arrangements."

"Not good enough," he repeated.

Her hand shook as she ran it through her hair. Her eyes prickled from the threat of sudden tears. "I thought you would want to be involved in the baby's life."

"Got it all figured out, don't you?" He frowned. "You walked away. Said we shouldn't ever have gotten married. If you felt that way, why'd you even want me to know you were pregnant?"

"Because even though our marriage didn't work out, you have the right to see your child. And because our baby has the right to a father."

She glared at him, daring him to disagree. She'd defend this baby she already loved. Would take on Father, Gabe, anyone. And she'd given Gabe the plain and simple truth. At least, part of it.

The only part he needed to know.

In answer, he rose and moved to stand a mere two feet away. His eyes glowed as he stared down at her. Funny. This close, melting caramel looked more like scorching-hot embers.

"Damn right, the baby needs a father—a full-time one."

Her heart thudded against her breast. She could barely breathe. Was he planning to fight for custody?

Gabe had the ranch. A steady income. A home.

She had nothing to give their child, nothing but love. That had to count for something.

"I told you I'm old-fashioned, Marissa. That means my child will be raised by two parents."

He moved closer.

She struggled to find her voice. "That would be difficult, considering the circumstances. I'll contact you after the baby's born, and—"

He moved even closer. Her heart leaped.

"Not good enough." He leaned forward, bending down until their noses nearly touched. His warm breath bathed her face.

Her throat closed so tightly she nearly choked. No matter how much she wanted their child to have a relationship with his or her father, she couldn't risk living with Gabe again.

She couldn't risk being near him, period.

He had seduced her, had made her feel loved for the first time in her life. But falling for him had reinforced her worst fears, too. The sexual attraction to him had swept her away and caused her to marry him. She had done what she had spent years swearing she would never do—follow in her mother's footsteps.

Already, with Gabe standing so close, she could feel herself weaken. She tried to step away, but the knob of the kitchen door pressed against her back.

"You don't think you can drop news like this and just take off again, do you? You don't think I'm letting you walk away with my child inside you?"

"You're not serious."

He loomed in front of her, wearing an uncompromising scowl. "About raising this baby together? Dead serious."

GABE KEPT HIS EYES on Marissa and told himself to harden his heart. As if he could actually get himself to do it.

Not likely, when he hadn't had the strength of will to leave her out in the cold, no matter how much he'd wanted her gone. She'd looked pale and shaken, as if she'd gone the distance on a bad-tempered bull. Just the way he felt with the double whammy she'd delivered.

Not yet divorced. And now, pregnant.

"Have a seat." He hooked the toe of his boot around the rung of a chair and pulled it closer to her. "You look like you need to get something in your stomach."

She paled further. "M-maybe just some toast. Dry toast."

Once she'd dropped into her seat, he cleared some dishes from the kitchen table and turned away. Without looking at her, he could almost breathe normally again.

"I could help myself." Her voice shook.

"Don't worry, I've got it." He took a plate down from the cupboard and dropped a slice of bread in the toaster. He remembered that she drank tea, and took a tea bag out of the tin.

He glanced at the back door just a few steps away. It was all he could do to keep himself from bolting out to the barn, saddling up Sunrise, and racing across his land. Anything to get away from facing this woman.

What the hell had spurred him to tell her they'd raise their kid together?

She'd been about to walk out on him. Yet again.

He'd gotten used to people leaving him. Employees who'd moved on, like the ranch foreman and his wife, who packed up just after Thanksgiving. Friends who'd decided they could find their fortune in some other town. His own mother…

He wouldn't think about that right now.

He moved mechanically, filling a pan with hot soapy water. Putting tea and toast on the table in front of Marissa.

"Thanks."

He grunted.

Now that he'd stopped moving, stopped feeling, he could take better stock. She looked as good as the day he'd met her, though the dark circles beneath her bright hazel eyes hadn't been there before. He remembered the silkiness of the light-brown hair swirling around her shoulders, wanted to feel it sliding between his fingers again.

Tearing his gaze away, he turned back to the sink, needing something to occupy his hands and his mind.

Damn, why hadn't he had Warren stay behind, like always? Giving the older man household chores since the ranch cook quit made Warren feel useful, as well as kept him from overworking himself. His old friend hadn't caught on yet. Gabe liked it that way. But, today, he'd sent Warren out with the others.

He'd needed time to deal with Marissa, to come to terms with her news.

Trouble was, his gut told him all the time in the world wouldn't help.

Behind him, he heard the crunch of dry toast, the clank of the teaspoon against the mug. "Gabe, I…need to use the facilities."

He shrugged. "Help yourself. The boys've been using the one off the kitchen. You might want to head upstairs."

"Thanks."

She crossed the room. He watched until she slipped through the doorway and her footsteps echoed on the stairs. He heard the echo of the words she'd said outside, too.

We're having a baby.

Not *I'm pregnant.* Or even, *I'm having a baby.* No, she had gone straight to the heart of the matter with just the right words. She was having *his* baby. And she wanted him to have a relationship with the child.

Or so she claimed.

Why hadn't she filed the divorce papers? Back then, to hear her tell it, she hadn't even known she was pregnant.

Ugly thoughts uncoiled in his gut.

Three months had gone by. In that time, she could have done anything, been with anyone. How could he be sure the baby was his?

Hell, how could he even know for sure she was pregnant?

It came down to him trusting her. But after all she

had done, all that had happened to him, trust was the one thing he didn't have.

He braced a hand against the edge of the sink and stared, almost unseeing, at the soapy water dripping from the dishcloth onto the floor.

"Gabe?"

With an effort, he turned his head. Marissa stood in the doorway, staring at him.

"Are you okay?"

"Tea's getting cold." He waved her toward the table and held his breath till she started that way. Getting her seated again would solve his problem for the moment.

He'd have to think of a way to keep her on the ranch.

Just long enough for him to find out what she was up to.

WARILY, Marissa moved across the kitchen to her chair again. She took a mouthful of tea.

And nearly choked on it when Gabe braced a hand on the table beside her and leaned in.

"You're my wife, Marissa. That right?"

"Yes," she managed, her insides like gelatin. But she kept her voice steady.

His voice alone had the power to thrill her. How could she share a house with him?

Yet even as panic flooded through her, part of her said staying might be the solution to one of her concerns. The key to resolving an issue from her past.

A way to prove she wasn't like her mother.

He sank into the adjacent seat and focused on her stomach. "That's my baby you're carrying?"

This time, she could only nod, and pray he didn't see the quiver shooting through her at his nearness.

"You said it yourself, the baby's got the right to a father."

"Of course."

"Okay, then. You don't have a job or a place to go. You can stay here until the baby comes."

"That's generous of you."

His eyes narrowed. "Generous, nothing. Just taking care of what's mine." One corner of his mouth curved upward, as if to soften his words. "You said, too, I have a right to my child."

"You do."

"And he won't be born the wrong side of the sheets. Stay here, stay married. I play the genuine husband. You act like the loving wife. And we both pretend the past three months never happened."

Her heart clenched. She didn't know what it meant to be a real wife. The disaster of their few weeks of marriage had proved that. And Lord knows, she didn't have any role models to follow. If she had, she might not have been caught in this no-win situation.

The baby would win.

She *had* to give the baby and Gabe a chance. Had to give them something better than her own disrupted childhood spent trailing along after her mother, while her father was left behind.

"My men can't know it's all a sham," he continued,

as if she'd already agreed to his plan. "I'd be a laughing-stock. Of course, that's something I've had to get used to since you left. I'm not going through that again. We'll pretend when we're with them, and out in public. And since we're both so old-fashioned—and still married—you'll move back into my bed."

"No." Shaking her head, she shot up from her chair.

Upstairs earlier, she'd fled past Gabe's bedroom—their bedroom, for such a short time.

"No," she repeated. "Sleeping together is not an option."

"Why not?"

Because I can't resist you.

And I'll die before I'll let you know it.

"What'll the boys all think?" he persisted.

"They live in the bunkhouse. They won't know I'm not sharing your bed."

The words made her heart ache, triggered memories of cuddling together in the king-size bed with the feather mattress and cozy quilt. Of falling asleep wrapped in Gabe's strong arms, and of waking up with their limbs entwined.

Except for the sleeping arrangements, what he offered now wasn't much different from the reality of their brief marriage. A sham from the beginning, built on sexual attraction, not love.

But they'd made a child together.

She swallowed hard. She'd longed for her parents to get together again. For them all to be a family and share a happy, stable home.

How could she deny those things to her child?

Slowly, she sank to her seat again. "All right. Maybe we can work this out. I'll act like the perfect wife. But I'm not making any promises."

She would stay. Not to sleep with him or give in to her attraction to him. Not even in the hopes of making him love her. She would stay because she had to do the right thing for their baby.

When he frowned, she knew he would never agree.

But a split second later, he nodded, and her fate was sealed.

Chapter Three

Gabe hauled the last of Marissa's suitcases into the guest room for her and set them on the bed beside the rest. Typical city girl, with a mess of luggage.

When they'd come home from Vegas he'd toted only a couple of suitcases up to their bedroom. But back then, she hadn't planned on getting married and moving to Dillon, Texas, inside of two weeks.

"Looks like this is the last of it." He took a light-weight carryall from his shoulder and dropped it onto the small pine chest.

"Thank you." She unzipped the bag, and he spied something soft and pink and lacy. The sight set his pulse to galloping—and sent him to the bedroom doorway.

"I've got work to do," he muttered.

She nodded.

He hightailed it out of the room, out of the house, and down to the barn.

He'd once liked a lot of things about Marissa. Her smile. Her changeable eyes. Her compact but curvy body. Listening to her when she talked and laughed. When she cried out as they'd made love.

And he'd damned sure liked taking off those soft, pink, lacy things she tended to wear to bed.

He wiped his brow and strode into the barn, where he found Warren up to his elbow in saddle soap.

The older man eyed him. "Everything okay?"

"Fine." He reached for a polishing cloth, worked it back and forth in his hands.

"The missus still up at the house?"

"Yep." Was she? A band of pressure tightened around his chest, and he flexed both arms, hoping for some relief.

"Big surprise, her just showing up like that."

"Yeah."

"She settling in again?"

"Uh-huh."

"Right talkative this morning, ain't you, boss?"

He gritted his teeth to hold back a sigh. Like a dog ferreting out a skunk—or a little old woman fishing for gossip—Warren wouldn't let up until Gabe had come out in the open.

Leaning sideways, he peered through the barn doorway. The Mustang still sat to one side of the driveway. The weight on his chest eased.

"Yeah, she's settling in again," he said. He might as well go whole hog to persuade Warren. Convince him, and the rest of the hands would follow. Then, with any luck, his friends and neighbors would, too. "It was all a misunderstanding, what happened before. We worked it out. She's staying." He nodded for emphasis. "Just needs a few days to get comfortable, get things sorted out."

"Nice that she's plannin' to stick around."

Was that doubt in Warren's voice? He'd fastened his squinted stare to the saddle in front of him.

The man's uncertainty didn't surprise him. His own faith in Marissa's staying power was as shaky as a newborn calf.

"Might be good to introduce her around a bit, boss, let her get to know folks." Warren looked sideways at him. "Reckon you'll be taking her to Doc's Christmas party this weekend."

His words sounded more like a statement than a question. It gave him pause.

Gabe hadn't planned on going to Doc's party himself—he'd kept close to home most of the time Marissa lived on the ranch and hadn't had much taste for gallivanting after she'd left.

Still, he'd made a deal with her about putting up a front. If they were going to pull this off, if she was really going to "settle in," he'd need to keep to the bargain. And already he was blowing it. He hadn't realized how hard he'd have to work at this playacting with Warren and the boys, or with all his neighbors and friends.

Well, there was one thing he could say that would satisfy Warren.

He clutched the polishing cloth and announced recklessly, "She's going to be taking over kitchen duties, starting with supper tonight."

"Yeah?"

Finally, a note of enthusiasm. Anything would be better than Gabe's so-called cooking.

The more he thought about the idea, the better it sounded. Having Marissa prepare the meals would free him up, keep his cowhands happy and reinforce the image of her as his loving wife.

And, most important of all, it would give him a way to keep her on the ranch.

UNABLE TO SIT STILL in the small guest room, Marissa reached for her suitcase. She had to do something to keep busy. Keep her hands—and her mind—occupied.

She had scheduled the detour to Texas as a side trip that would last about an hour. Never had she expected to be staying here. But, one look at Gabe's light brown eyes, and she was caught up in the magic again.

She hadn't been able to resist him. Wistfully, she recalled how he had "propositioned" her, so to speak, just minutes after they'd met.

She couldn't think about that. Those magical days were over.

Fine. She had so much more to consider now.

For the baby's sake, she would stay here and find the strength of will to resist Gabe. She would prove she was nothing like her mother.

A knock sounded behind her. Startled, she whirled, clutching a handful of items from the suitcase.

"Gabe! What are you doing here?"

"Looking for you. What else?"

His eyes were riveted to a spot at her midriff. She looked down to find her hands overflowing with silk bras and panties, then looked up and saw the heat in his eyes. She felt an answering warmth flush her cheeks.

"D-did you need something?"

"Yeah." He nearly growled the word.

She stood frozen for a long moment, knowing what could so easily happen between them right then. What had so easily and so often happened in the past. And what she had to avoid at all costs until she knew where she stood.

"Why don't we talk in the kitchen?" she suggested. "I'll be there in just a minute."

He nodded and walked away. She flushed again, realizing how caught up in memories she must have been, not to have heard his steady footsteps approaching. She had to leave all those memories behind her, where they belonged. She'd have to be on her guard.

Exhaling, she dropped the undergarments onto the bed and followed Gabe's path. She settled into the familiar chair near the kitchen door.

Gabe came to sit opposite her. "You can take on some chores around here."

She frowned. "Since when do you decide things for me?"

"I'm not deciding. I'm making you an offer."

"It sure doesn't sound like that to me. Why don't you just ask me, instead of giving me an order?"

He looked at her in obvious confusion. "I *am* asking."

She gave up. "What is it?"

"I want you to take on some cooking duties."

"Oh, really? Why? Did Mary go on strike?" In her short time on the ranch, Marissa had met—and done her best to avoid—the cook, who'd made it plain she needed no help from an outsider.

"They moved back East with their kids and grandkids."

They, she recalled, included the cook's husband, who had some kind of management job on Gabe's ranch.

"I don't know much about your kitchen," she told him. "I tended to stay away since Mary told me I was 'a mite different from the last woman of the house.'" She waited, but of course Gabe said nothing. He had never said much about his family life. She wondered what his mother had been like, how much she had done to shape Gabe into the man he was today.

In her case, her father's money had helped shape her, though Gabe didn't know about that.

What he had known very well, though—and had just as likely forgotten—was the fact that she was trained as a chef. They had met in Las Vegas only because she had been in town for a cooking convention. He had probably forgotten that, too.

She lived to cook. Loved to cook. But it wouldn't hurt to keep quiet until she got a better idea of what Gabe wanted.

"You said *some* cooking duties?" she repeated.

"Yeah. Breakfast and supper."

"Not lunch?"

"Nah. Give you a break on that."

"You're too kind," she said drily. "The men don't usually come in from the ranch at lunchtime, do they?"

"That's right." He paused. "So, you up for it?"

"I don't know." She said it slowly, not wanting to make things too easy for him.

"C'mon." He added, "The bunkhouse kitchen's all set up with a six-burner stove and industrial-size icebox."

"It is?" Much better suited for cooking for a crowd. And for preparing some of her more complicated menus.

"Only decent meals you'll get around here is if you cook 'em yourself."

"Hmm...well, in that case—"

"Great! The boys'll be tickled to hear the news."

When he rose and turned away, Marissa couldn't hold back a grin.

She certainly wanted to eat healthy, nourishing meals for the baby. She really needed something to occupy her during the long, lonely days on the ranch.

And she desperately needed something—someone—to run interference between her and Gabe. Warren and the rest of the cowboys would do the trick. She couldn't have planned anything more perfect herself.

"Everything you need's either in this kitchen or the other." He took a sheepskin jacket from a peg on the wall and pulled open the door. Sunshine and chilly air filled the kitchen. "See you at suppertime."

"I'll be ready," she promised.

"Me, too, honey." He gave her a grin that chased all

the cold air away. "Ready for putting on a good show for the boys."

LATE THAT AFTERNOON, looking at the pots simmering on the stove, Marissa frowned.

As a chef, she had prepared banquets for hundreds, yet she felt more nervous about serving this first simple meal.

Simple was the key word, all right. She had found the refrigerator bare except for some breakfast staples, and the pantry sadly lacked in variety.

Well, she'd made do and hoped they would enjoy it.

She wanted this dinner to go well. It was the first time she would be sitting down to eat with them all.

In the weeks she had spent here in September, the ranch hands and Mary had taken their meals in this bunkhouse kitchen. The cook had left covered dishes, kept warm in the oven, at the main house.

Gabe and Marissa hadn't lingered long over these meals. Instead, they had retired early in the evenings to his bedroom....

She forced her mind back to her dinner.

When the kitchen door opened, she took a deep breath and turned to greet her dinner companions. The first man strode into the kitchen—Gabe.

He had obviously just showered and changed into clean clothes. The crisp white Western shirt made his hair look darker than ever. With an effort, she shifted her attention and smiled at the handful of men who had crowded into the open doorway behind him.

It looked like they wore fresh shirts, too, as if they'd

dressed for a special occasion. She was touched by the effort. Maybe they were as nervous about this first meal as she was.

For a minute, they all stood staring at one another.

The oldest of the bunch, Warren, broke the silence. He rubbed his hands together energetically. "Whoo-hoo—something's smelling mighty good around here."

The other men chorused agreement.

"What can we do to help, missus?"

Warren's offer broke the ice, and soon he and the younger men were pouring drinks and transferring bowls of hot food to the table.

Amid all the bustle, she'd lost sight of Gabe. A moment later, when he appeared next to her at the stove, she nearly jumped.

"Did you forget something, honey?" he asked in a low, intimate tone guaranteed to set her pulse soaring.

She looked pointedly from him to the neatly set oak table, then back to him. "No, I don't think so."

He slid an arm around her waist and cupped his hand around her hip. Warmth started where his fingers touched. It spread out and down and through her.

"How about a kiss for your hardworking husband?"

She shot a look over her shoulder. A conversation had broken out at the table, and all eyes focused on one of the men sitting at the opposite end of the room.

"At the moment, your acting skills aren't necessary," she hissed at Gabe, keeping her voice down. "No one's paying a bit of attention to us." Sidestepping, she lifted a bowl of peas from the stove. "Would you set this on the table, please?"

He didn't move.

She thrust the bowl toward him. Smiling, she shifted closer, letting his body block her completely from everyone's view. Then she glared at him. "Two choices, Gabe Miller," she murmured. "Take the bowl of peas. Or clean up the mess from the floor."

His hands were instantly beneath the bowl. But as he removed it from her grasp, he leaned forward and skimmed her mouth with his.

She couldn't call it a kiss, only a brief brush of their lips, but the friction zinged straight down to her toes.

He grinned. "Always happy to oblige a lady."

He obliged her, all right, whenever it came to a meeting of bodies. And she couldn't do a thing to resist him. Yet he had no trouble resisting her when it came to a meeting of the minds.

She moved on unsteady legs to slip into a vacant chair between Warren and another man.

Gabe raised a brow but managed to keep any other expression from showing. He took a seat at the opposite end of the table and pulled a dish of Duchess potatoes toward him.

Staring at her, he said, "Looks tempting."

"Thank you." She hoped the men would attribute her burning cheeks to standing so close to the stove.

"Gotta beat Gabe's cooking," said the tallest, lankiest cowboy, a redhead with scattered freckles and a wide grin.

"Watch it, Hank," Gabe warned. But he laughed.

"Hank fancies himself the next best thing to a stand-up comedian," he said good-naturedly.

Warren turned to her, his face serious. "I told the boss me and the boys were grateful to have you here."

Voices rang out around them.

"Sure are."

"Yep."

"Got that right."

"Thank you," she told them all, fighting to keep wistfulness from her tone.

She didn't need gratitude from Gabe, but she couldn't help wishing he was happy to have her there, and as something other than a means of restoring his reputation.

Avoiding his eye, she said, "It sounds like Gabe isn't much of a cook."

Hank guffawed. "Ma'am, that's about like saying a coyote doesn't make for a very good pet."

She laughed as the others chimed in.

As they continued eating their dinner, any shyness Marissa might have felt around the men dissolved. They alternately complimented her cooking and tried to outdo each other with tales of Gabe's worst moments in the kitchen.

"Food's important to a man," Eddie, a young cowboy, told her. "Specially when he's gotta be out on the range all day in this freezing weather."

"Yeah," added Jared, a quieter, dark-haired man. "And especially when he's a growing boy who can't get his fill of sweet things."

"And they aren't all women."

"Hank!" Gabe snapped.

Hank looked at Marissa. "'Scuse me, ma'am. No disrespect meant."

"None taken." She smiled at Eddie, who couldn't have been more than eighteen. "You're in luck. Desserts are one of my specialties." In fact, she had spent time in Switzerland being mentored by a renowned pastry chef. "I'll see what I can do about your sweet tooth."

"Gee, thanks, ma'am." Eddie turned red and ducked his head.

"About time we cleared out of here," Gabe announced.

Her feeling of contentment dissolved as quickly as her shyness had such a short while before. Did Gabe intend to get a goodbye kiss from her—in front of all of his men—before he left with them?

Or, worse, did he plan to stay here with her after they were gone?

Her palms grew damp, and she felt rooted to her seat.

The cowboys gave her polite thanks for the meal and began to trickle from the room.

"Don't mind the boys." Warren hovered near the open door. "Cowhands usually come a bit rough round the edges."

"That's okay, Warren. Thank you."

She smiled at him, temporarily forgetting her worries about Gabe. He bobbed his head and shuffled through the doorway.

As Gabe pushed the door closed, cold air whooshed around her. Her worries whooshed back, too. She shivered.

"Cold?" he asked, moving around his end of the table.

"Just fine." She jumped up from her seat and began collecting dishes to carry to the sink.

"Think so?"

"What do you mean?"

"That performance you put on in front of my men. Or didn't put on, more like it."

"I promised to act like your wife—"

"Loving wife."

"Like your wife," she repeated, glaring at him. "But I'll tell you this, Gabe Miller. I am not going to swoon and fall into your arms every time you look at me."

"Why not?" He frowned. "You sure used to, once upon a time."

She plopped the dishes on the counter.

He must have seen the fire in her eyes. "Hey, simmer down. I'm only—"

"And one more thing." She had gone way beyond the simmering stage. An overreaction, maybe, but the months apart from him had given her plenty of time to reach a full, rolling boil. "If you expect me to continue with this game we're playing, you'll keep from using our past against me."

He yanked the door open again. "Fine load of double-talk, Marissa." His mouth curled in disgust. "If not for our past, you wouldn't be here."

Hatless and coatless, he stalked out, slamming the

door behind him. The window over the sink rattled. Marissa sank into the nearest chair.

Like it or not, Gabe was right. On both counts.

In the days when they had first met, every time he'd looked at her, she had just about come undone. Every time he'd moved close to her, she'd felt a rush of energy and excitement that overwhelmed her. Every time he'd touched her—

No, she couldn't think of that.

The fact that he knew these things, that he would willingly remind her of them, hurt her almost as much as her own shame.

The fact that they were just as true now as they'd been three and a half months ago hurt her, too.

Sighing, she wrapped her arms around herself, cradling her stomach. She'd come back for all the right reasons—she had to keep telling herself that.

This fighting couldn't be good for the baby. It had to stop. She had made the agreement with Gabe, and now she had to stand by it with as little tension as possible.

The only way to do that was to stay out of Gabe's way as much as she could.

Chapter Four

Marissa rinsed cucumbers and set them on the butcher-block countertop in the bunkhouse kitchen. She made a mental note not to put any in Hank's salad.

Before, when she'd stayed on the ranch, she'd had almost no contact with any of the cowboys. But now, after only two days back, they seemed to have accepted her. And she'd already come to know many of their food likes and dislikes.

Her queasy stomach and sensitivity to certain smells seemed to give her trouble only early in the mornings. A good thing, because she needed to cook, to do what she loved.

Her new duties helped ease the loneliness she had felt the first time she'd lived with Gabe. And she felt more at home in both kitchens than she did anywhere else on the ranch.

She heard heavy footsteps crunching gravel, approaching the bunkhouse.

Gabe.

She had told herself she would avoid him when she could, keep her distance when she couldn't. He had made that easy for her.

In the two days since she had returned to Dillon, he had spent most of his time working, just as he had in the days following their marriage. The days she had felt so alone.

Other than meals, she had hardly had to see him at all. When they did meet, there was no more fighting between them, but the tension remained high.

Her breath caught in her throat when he stepped through the doorway.

He wasn't the tallest man she'd ever met, but he made a mouthwatering picture. He'd rolled the sleeves of his Western shirt to his elbows, showing strong forearms dusted with dark hair. His lower body was encased in a pair of well-worn jeans, faded to white in all the important places.

Rugged. Solid. And much too sexy.

Clearing her throat, she grabbed a knife and a tomato and began chopping. "You're in early," she said, hoping he couldn't hear the waver in her voice.

"You noticed."

She risked a sideways glance.

The ends of his hair, still damp from his shower, lay dark against his tanned neck. A faint scent of his woodsy aftershave drifted over to her.

The memories connected to that scent slammed home. Their meeting at her hotel in Las Vegas. Their wagon ride beneath the southern stars. Their many times making love.

Her hands trembled and her knees felt weak, yet Gabe hadn't made a move to touch her.

She berated herself for her fantasies. For the reactions she couldn't seem to control whenever he was near.

Nervousness loosened her tongue. "You know, I'm glad we've come to this arrangement—the cooking, I mean. It's my...favorite job."

She'd almost said "passion" but caught herself, knowing she shouldn't use that word—shouldn't *think* that word—anywhere around this man.

Trying to make her movements casual, she lifted the cutting board and stepped away from him.

He edged nearer, closing in.

"Besides," she blurted, "cooking for your cowboys gives me the satisfaction of having something to do. Who knew I'd wind up in charge of your meals? It's certainly a switch from when I was here before."

"When I was never around, so you said."

"Well, that was true."

"Daytimes, yeah. I had to be away. But the nights were different, weren't they?"

She remained silent, stirring the contents of the Dutch oven and wishing he would find a reason to leave.

"Ranch cook's a heck of a comedown for a big-city chef, huh?"

She smiled. "I'm surprised you remembered what I did for a living, other than working in a hotel."

"I remember a lot of things. You were taking a cooking class when I met you in Vegas."

"Yes." When he'd swept her off her feet. Heavenly days, followed by long, lonely weeks on this ranch. But as he'd said, the nights… She couldn't think about the nights.

"I've been cooking since I was tall enough to reach the front burners," she blurted to keep the subject neutral. "It's practically second nature to me now."

"Your mom teach you?"

"No. I taught myself." Her mother's skills weren't in the kitchen. "My parents are divorced. When I was sixteen, I went to New York City to live with my father. He owned a restaurant or two." Or two dozen. "By then, I already knew my way around a kitchen and loved to cook. Father agreed to send me for advanced classes."

Over the years, she had earned outstanding grades, a job as head chef in his Chicago restaurant and, at last and just lately, his grudging acceptance. She didn't want to think about the strain her news would put on their already troubled relationship.

Gabe strolled over to stand beside her, so close she couldn't tell where the heat from the stove ended and the warmth of his body began.

"Mmm, stew." The words were uttered in a sexy growl.

Looking away, she stirred the tomatoes, watching as they turned to pulp. The way her insides were feeling.

"Smells good. The boys'll like it."

"I—I hope so."

She was salivating over Gabe and the only thing on his mind was her cooking. Not long ago, she would have been insulted. Now, she simply felt relieved. His lack of interest in her reminded her she was only playing a part. Happy homemaker. Perfect wife. She took a deep breath and tried to think of something to say that would fit her role.

"I wanted to make Beef Bourguignonne with chestnuts, but neither of your kitchens came stocked with mushrooms or red wine. Or chestnuts, for that matter."

"The boys don't need anything fancy. They're happy enough having you in the kitchen."

"They won't be happy when I run out of things to feed them."

He didn't answer. He stared across the room, his brow ridged in a frown. Though he didn't look her way, she was all too aware of his broad body filling the space between the oak table and the stove. Of his bare forearms, the V at the neck of his shirt, the tiny white creases at the outside corners of his eyes....

She needed breathing space. Badly.

With a shaking hand, she placed the lid on the Dutch oven and lowered the flame beneath it. "This has to simmer for a few hours. I...I need to go into town to do some shopping. I'll be back in time."

Still, he didn't answer, didn't budge.

"Gabe."

Finally, he turned his head to look at her, his eyes seeming to focus from a long way off.

"What?"

"I'm going for groceries. The stew can sit for a while." She sidled past the stove, trying not to brush against him. "I'll see you at dinner."

She rushed across the kitchen, fumbled with the doorknob and yanked open the door.

Safe.

Until she heard her name.

"Hold on a minute," Gabe said. "I'll run you into town."

GABE PUSHED the overloaded cart through the doors of the market. At this rate, he'd need to sell off a calf or two long before the next roundup.

They stopped at his pickup in the parking lot. "You sure you got everything you need?"

"Mmm-hmm."

"Must not be the selection you're used to in the big city."

"No, but I'll manage."

Beside him, she leaned over to lift a couple of milk jugs from the cart. Her swirl of hair swept across one shoulder. Her jeans pulled tight over the curve of her hips.

Underneath the brim of his Stetson, sweat broke out. He swallowed a groan and grabbed a few sacks.

She looked up, her hazel eyes glowing like polished silver in the sunshine. "I told you you didn't have to bring me to town. And you certainly didn't have to come shopping with me."

"No problem."

"Then why are you scowling at me?" She placed the milk jugs in the truck. "Ever since we left the ranch, you've looked like you swallowed a mouthful of lemon zest. What's wrong?"

"Nothing." Grumbling under his breath, he finished

loading the sacks into the pickup. *Zest.* He didn't want to talk about *zest.*

He'd seen plenty enough of that lately with the downright fawning his cowhands had done over her since she'd taken on the cooking.

Good thing he didn't have a jealous streak, or it would've flowed wider than the Rio Grande.

It riled him, though. Having Marissa do the cooking was supposed to give credence to the idea of their happy marriage. Warren and the hands didn't seem to notice whether the bride and groom acted like newlyweds or not. They'd accepted her, befriended her and, come mealtime, sat licking their chops over whatever she piled on their plates.

What was that old saying, something about getting people to eat out of your hands? Did she have an ulterior motive for trying to win over his men? By finding a way to keep her on the ranch, had he played right into her scheme?

He'd have to change his tactics. Instead of avoiding her by working double hard, he'd stick by her side. Keep a close watch. Find out what she was up to.

"Good afternoon, Gabe."

The familiar soft-spoken voice tore him from his thoughts. He turned and tipped his Stetson to the woman. She'd once towered over him; now he had to lean down to kiss her wrinkled cheek.

"Hey, Mrs. G. Good to see you."

"You, too. It's been a while, Gabe Miller." Behind her wire-framed glasses, her eyes looked sideways.

He did the same, in time to catch Marissa give the older woman a small smile, then shoot a glance his way, as if she wanted him to make the next move. So he did.

He wrapped an arm around her shoulders.

She stiffened but, to his surprise, didn't pull away.

It had been a long time since he'd held her. Much as he hated to think it, he missed having her beside him. She felt good there. Too good. Her soft curves brushed against him, turning his insides all warm. He had to fight to remember where they stood. To warn himself that he couldn't trust her.

"Uh...Mrs. G, this is my wife, Marissa. Honey, Mrs. Gannett taught school here in Dillon. And had me standing in a corner of the play yard more times than I care to admit."

Both women laughed.

"Nice to meet you." As she leaned forward to shake hands, Marissa shifted away from him.

He resettled his grip, sliding his arm down a little, cuddling her to his side again. He had the right—they were married, weren't they?

And with his suspicions about her motives stronger than ever, he would make damn sure she stayed close at hand.

Mrs. G smiled. "I'm retired now. But Dillon's a very small town, so I see a great deal of my former students. Though I'd heard he married, Gabe's done a good job of keeping his bride to himself." She turned to him. "I'm sure we'll be seeing you both at Doc's?"

"Doc's?" he asked.

"The annual Christmas potluck?"

"Oh, yeah." First Warren, and now Mrs. G, had mentioned his taking Marissa to Doc's. He considered. Everyone in town showed up for the party. He couldn't ask for a better way of introducing her around and cementing their relationship in people's minds before a baby came along.

"Sure. We'll look for you on Saturday, all right. Wouldn't miss it. Isn't that right, honey?"

"That's right." She smiled.

"We won't keep you, Mrs. G. You probably want to get your shopping done."

"Well…"

"And we've got a load of frozen groceries to get home."

She nodded. "See you Saturday, then. We'll have a nice chat, Marissa. I look forward to getting to know you."

With his free hand, he tipped his Stetson and smiled. Once Mrs. G had left, he steered Marissa toward the end of the truck.

As soon as they rounded the corner, she pulled away from his arm. Instantly, he missed the pressure of her curves against him. "Hey! No need to run off so quick."

"We're alone now," she said through clenched teeth. "And there was never a need for the armlock you had me in…*honey*."

He laughed. "Just being husbandly. Like we said, remember?" He reached up to stroke her jaw.

She backed against the side of the pickup and stared at him.

He frowned. "Don't tell me you forgot our agreement."

"Of course, I didn't forget. I just gave a stellar performance, don't you think?"

"Sure do." He stepped forward, till his chest brushed the front of her jacket. It wasn't close enough. "Just like we said," he reminded her. "Pretend we're happily married when we're in public. With the power of Dillon's grapevine, this little outing of ours ought to make it around town triple time."

He glanced over at the market. Sure enough, Mrs. G stood just inside the picture window, along with a group of other shoppers. Most of them were townsfolk who'd spent the past three months trying to hide their pity. He turned back to the woman who'd made all his friends feel sorry for him.

"Seems that the curtain's still up and the audience is waiting, Marissa. Let's show 'em this marriage is for real."

He looked into her upturned face.

Suddenly, it didn't matter who was watching and who wasn't, what they saw or what they thought. All that mattered stood right in front of him, her hazel eyes soft in the shadow of his Stetson. He wanted to hold her in his arms again, bury his hands in her hair.

Her lips parted, but before she could say a word, he dipped his head and swept her into a heart-stopping kiss.

Chapter Five

For the thousandth time in two days, Marissa brushed a finger across her lips, reliving the memory of how Gabe's mouth had caressed hers. He had sent up more flames inside her than a match set to the bunkhouse's gas stove. And she had welcomed the warming blaze.

She craved his kiss, wanted his attention, hoped it would be proved there was more to him than the indifferent man who worked so hard out on the ranch and then came home and ignored her.

Foolish hopes, of course.

In truth, his kiss—and her response—only underscored the fool she'd made of herself by marrying him. By mistaking sexual chemistry for love.

And if she didn't stop dwelling on it, she would get burned again.

Desperate for a distraction, she glanced around the living room. It looked just the way it had the first time she'd seen it, months before, all browns and rusts and leathers. The furniture sat in the same places. Ranching and farming magazines overflowed the wooden box in one corner. Warm and cozy, and just a bit shabby. A man's room. Gabe's room. Never hers.

Just as he had never been hers. And still wasn't.

Her heart ached.

Yet, she couldn't keep from closing her eyes, from cuddling the afghan in her arms closer to her, and from daydreaming. A baby. A family. Gabe...

"Marissa."

"Mmm-hmm?" Drowsily, she responded to his whisper.

Then she realized he'd muttered her name, not whispered it. And that the word wasn't a figment of her imagination, but the very real sound of his voice. Her eyes popped open.

"Gabe!"

He stood in the living-room entry, leaning against the frame.

In the two days since their trip to the market...since their kiss, she had seen more of him than in all the days following their wedding combined.

At this moment, in a manner of speaking, she saw even more.

Soft lamplight made his day's growth of beard shimmer, his brown eyes shine. He had pulled his Western shirt out of the waistband of his jeans. Snaps undone, the shirtfront hung open, two panels of stark-white fabric teasing her with a glimpse of tanned skin and a sprinkling of dark hair.

Her throat tightened, and she sank to the leather couch.

"You were expecting someone else?" he asked.

"No. I wasn't expecting anyone at all. You startled me." With trembling hands, she shook out the afghan and made a production of folding it into a neat oblong across her lap. "I thought you'd gone upstairs for the night."

"I wanted to talk to you about the party tomorrow."

Her hands stilled on the afghan. She couldn't go to a party with him. No matter what agreement they had come to, she wouldn't make it through socializing with his friends and neighbors for hours, with him standing by her side.

"At Doc's," he continued. "Mrs. G talked about it the other day, remember?"

She remembered, all right—it was just before their farce in front of his former schoolteacher and a storefront filled with people. His acting so...so "husbandly," as he had called it. No question—he had his role down pat.

"Christmas party," he added now.

Seeing a way out, she said, "We don't have any gifts."

He shrugged. "Don't need any. It's just a potluck."

"I don't have the ingredients for any of my specialties."

"So tomorrow morning, you can visit the market again."

"I don't have anything to wear."

"Jeans and a shirt." He raised his arms, indicating his attire. The shirtfront spread apart, giving her an almost full view of his chiseled chest.

She felt herself blanch. From his suggestion, that was all. "It's a Christmas party, Gabe. Jeans aren't appropriate."

He rolled his eyes. "City gals."

"Meaning what?" She frowned. This wasn't the first time he'd mentioned something about the city.

"Always wanting to dress up."

"You seemed to like it in Las Vegas."

"That was Vegas. This is Dillon, Texas, and out here, we don't need to go putting on airs."

"Putting on—" Standing, she threw down the afghan. "Are you trying to say I'm a snob?" *Like her father.*

"No."

"Then what? That I'm not good enough?" *Lower-class. Like her mother.* True as the thought was, the un-kindness of it made her wince. "That I won't fit in with your friends?"

"Whoa. Easy, now—"

"I might be a city mouse, Gabe, but I'm as good as *any* country mouse, *any* day."

"Mouse?" Eyes wide, he stared at her. "What the hell are you talking about?"

"It's a children's story. You wouldn't understand."

"You're right about that." He shook his head again and began backing out of the doorway. "I'm turning in for the night."

"Good."

For once, the thought of him going alone to the bed they'd shared months ago didn't have the power to distract her.

Exhaling through her teeth, she glared at the empty doorway.

She hadn't meant to explode at him, but his sudden

attentiveness had made their situation almost unbearable for her during the past two days. Worse, she still had to face meals with him in the company of Warren and the cowboys.

They barely noticed the interplay between their boss and his wife. Yet Gabe had insisted they stay in their roles.

And her ability to resist him was weakening.

Shame burned her cheeks. She *had* to prove she wouldn't just give in to any man who showed any interest in her at all.

Unwanted memories washed over her….

The years of living with her mother, of being hauled along like baggage, of falling behind in yet another one of her classes as they moved from city to city. Apartment to apartment. As her mother moved from man to man.

Finally, at sixteen, Marissa had rebelled. After one too many times of locking her bedroom door to keep her mother's latest boyfriend out, she had taken desperate measures.

First, the loan of enough money from her mother's purse to buy herself a bus ticket to New York. Then, her arrival on her father's doorstep unannounced.

The money had been her mother's "gift" from the current boyfriend, who would not have appreciated the irony. The girl whose bedroom door he had been unable to pry open had used him as her means of escape.

Leaving her mother and the boyfriend behind had been much easier than getting Father to agree to let her move in with him.

"You'll have to redeem yourself scholastically, Marissa," he had said in frozen tones from behind his polished executive desk.

He looked like an emperor on his throne, with his regal gestures and distant manner. Marissa would live by her father's rules. She wanted a safe place to live, nothing more. The less she expected, the smaller the disappointment. Life with her mother had taught her that.

"I'll catch up, Father," she promised. "I brought my English grammar book and my—"

"You will need to develop a good work ethic. A place in one of my restaurant kitchens might suit you."

"Oh, yes," she said, ecstatic at his sudden kindness.

Although she had envisioned running the restaurant kitchen, the manager gave her the job of peeling vegetables. She had taken on the menial chore gladly, working hard every day in the noisy preparation room off the main kitchen. With money from her first paycheck, she anonymously mailed to her mother the exact amount she had borrowed.

She also worked relentlessly to meet Father's standards at the girls' prep school he sent her to. As the months rolled by, she pulled her grades up to match, then exceed, those of her classmates. She wasn't sure who was more surprised, Father or herself, when she graduated with honors.

Then, in the first sign she had seen of his acceptance of her, it was off to college and the top cooking schools in the United States and Europe. A job in his Chicago restaurant. A convention in Las Vegas.

And a chance meeting with a Texas cowboy, the sexiest man she had ever seen.

A man she was now married to.

Gabe's announcement about the neighborhood Christmas party—about the need to act like newlyweds in front of a roomful of strangers—had set her nerves on edge.

His reference to her as a city girl had struck a raw place inside her, too. Moving from her mother's ragtag existence to her father's world of moneyed luxury had left her feeling she didn't fit into either setting. Gabe's unfortunate comment seemed to say this was yet another place she didn't belong.

She'd show him.

She would go to that Christmas party. Would act like the perfect wife. Meet all his friends. And keep herself so busy, she'd barely notice Gabe's body next to hers all night long.

Then she'd show him what a city mouse could do. Armed with her fanciest entrées, her most elegant desserts, her white-chocolate-truffles-to-die-for, she'd wow every one of his neighbors.

She'd knock Gabe's socks— No.

She'd knock that cowboy right off his hand-tooled, spit-shined, tanned-leather booted heels.

BRINGING MARISSA to this party wasn't the best idea he'd ever had.

From his stance by the buffet table, Gabe took another swig of holiday punch, hoping to soothe his parched throat and ease the tension tightening his jaw.

No matter how he tried to stop himself, no matter how many other bodies filled the room, his attention unerringly homed in on one particular body.

Doc had gone all out on decorations for his annual party, with help from Mrs. G and Delia from the diner. Still, the prettiest thing in the place, to his mind, was Marissa.

She stood with a group near the Christmas tree. Twinkling lights reflected off her long hair and her sparkly green dress. Her smile lit up the room.

He frowned. During the past few days, he'd run with his plan and stuck close to her. She hadn't done anything, said anything, to give him a better handle on her scheme. Except for those crazy notions she'd spouted when he'd invited her to the party.

He shook his head. He'd never understand women.

Look at her now. He'd been prepared to act the perfect husband, introduce her around, get her settled in.

But, since their arrival at Doc's, she hadn't needed his help. Heck, the way folks'd all taken to her, she might've known them for twenty years. The shyness he'd seen outside the market had disappeared faster than the punch he was guzzling.

The market. Holding her had felt good. Kissing her had felt even better. For a pretend marriage, it sure as hell seemed real to him. And that's what had brought him to his senses.

He wouldn't let his attraction to a woman run roughshod over his good judgment. Again.

He'd just keep playing his role, get himself over

there right up next to her. But he wouldn't let her throw another spell over him.

"Life of the party." The voice at his elbow made him swing around. His host, Doc Thompson, stood eyeing him.

"She sure is, isn't she?" Gabe said.

Doc laughed. "I was talking about you, son."

"You caught me." He couldn't help grinning at the man who'd brought him into this world.

Tall, white haired, and roughly the shape of Santa, Doc favored fancy vests under his medical jacket. Tonight, in keeping with the season, a row of elves paraded across the man's belly.

"You know me well enough, Doc. Know I'm never looking to impress anybody."

"Except that little gal, maybe?"

"Hmmph. Can't make an impression when she won't stand still."

"I reckon I can see what kept her on the move today." Doc reached for Gabe's glass to refill it. "She sure fixed up a mess of things, didn't she? That chicken dish specially hit the spot."

Gabe looked down the table at Marissa's contributions, the casseroles and plates now almost emptied. He couldn't hold back a burst of pride, though he hated himself for letting it show. Well, hell, it would fit his role, anyhow. "This is only half of it, Doc. The desserts are all lined up in the kitchen."

"So Lily Gannett said. Your Marissa sure is one popular lady with her."

"Yeah." And with everyone else at the party. And Warren. And the rest of his employees.

Doc nodded. "Now, son, you know I'm not one for advising on someone's personal business—"

"Ha," he interrupted. "Doc, you're a disgrace to your profession, telling such whoppers. Hey, Kev." Gabe grabbed the suspenders of a young boy who had just hustled past them, bringing him to a halt. "Let me ask you something. Doc here ever tell you what to do when you have a loose tooth?"

"Sure. He said leave it be. If they fall out on their own, the Tooth Fairy will bring me more money."

"Aha. And was Doc right?"

"Yep."

"Thanks, Kev. See you later."

The boy scampered off toward a group near the kiddie table.

Brows raised, Gabe looked again at the man beside him. "Proof positive, Doc. You told me—and every other kid in town—the same story. Giving advice goes along with your white coat. Always has."

The older man laughed and shrugged. "Well, don't you think I've earned the right?" He put a hand on Gabe's shoulder and turned suddenly serious. "Gabe, all I've got to say is, after a lifetime taking care of this town, I know just about everybody—and their history, to boot. Including you and yours."

"No argument from me there."

"Then I hope you'll take this in the spirit it's intended. The Christmas spirit, as a matter of fact." Doc finally handed him his drink. "Don't let what happened long ago keep you from living your life."

Gabe gripped the glass with suddenly sweaty fingers and fought a flash of memory. For a heartbeat, he became a boy Kevin's age again. A boy who'd climbed onto his daddy's knee to learn his mama had left him.

He'd never forget that day. Never forgive her.

Just as he'd never forgive Marissa.

He looked at her again, at the way that sparkly green dress skimmed over her, flowed down her flat belly.

Was she really carrying his child?

If he knew for certain, he'd know better how to handle the matter. Yes, she was pregnant, and he'd find a way to keep her on the ranch till the baby was born and they could figure things out from there. No, she wasn't, and he'd kick her off his land for good.

The thought struck him that there were tests Doc could run that would give him the answers he needed. He turned to his old friend and came a second away from spilling his guts. Then he thought twice.

He'd swallowed enough pity from the people in this room. He didn't need any more. He'd just have to wait and see what developed.

As he'd told Marissa nearly a week ago.

Uncertainty soured his stomach. His disposition, too.

"I thought you invited me here for a party, Doc. Now I'm wondering if I should look for a bill in the mail."

"No, son, tonight the checkup comes free." Doc clapped him on the shoulder, then moved away.

With a glance across the room, he saw Marissa laughing at something one of the women had said.

After one long, glass-draining gulp of punch, he flicked his left thumb against his wedding band.

Back at the house, he'd seen the flash of gold on Marissa's finger and had hightailed it up to his room for his own ring. A prop for the part he had to play.

It was showtime.

Chapter Six

Doc Thompson, their host, had taken Marissa under his wing.

She liked the older man, from his bright gray eyes and benevolent smile to the group of elves cavorting across his midsection.

With a sense of old-fashioned charm, he had escorted her into the house. Before she knew it, she had been surrounded by a group of his guests.

Later, Mrs. Gannett picked up where Doc left off. In her soft, sweet voice, Gabe's former teacher proceeded to introduce her to anyone who happened by. It seemed that was almost everyone.

"You're the hit of the party, my dear," Mrs. Gannett told her, patting her arm. "Mark my words, the ladies will start lining up at your door for your recipes."

Marissa smiled in pleasure. "They're welcome to them."

A rancher's wife she had met earlier approached them. "'Scuse me, Lily, do you have a minute?" She began talking in a low tone, and Marissa stepped away to give them some privacy.

The compliments to her cooking thrilled her. So did Gabe's absence. She hadn't trusted his intentions for this party one bit.

Instead of staying glued to her side, as she had feared he would, they had each gone their separate ways upon their arrival. Still, all evening, she had felt his gaze on her, as direct and tangible as a touch.

Once Doc swept her into the party, she had kept busy enough to ignore the unwelcome urge to seek Gabe out. Until now.

She spotted him near the buffet table, deep in conversation with Doc and a seven-year-old. She had already met and immediately liked the adorable Kevin Jones and his mother, Sarah.

Mrs. Gannett touched her arm. "Excuse me, Marissa, I'm wanted in the kitchen."

Marissa nodded in farewell. At the nearby children's table, a squabble broke out. She looked in that direction, wondering if she should intervene. But Sarah Jones was on the scene sorting things out before Marissa could take a step.

She sighed. If only she could find someone to solve her own problems.

She risked another fleeting glance toward the buffet table.

Trouble came loping toward her.

Gabe's mouth curved up at one corner. His eyes locked with hers. She wanted to move away but couldn't convince her feet to cooperate. He came to a stop in front of her.

"Enjoying your—?" He paused to greet Sarah, who seemed to have settled the dispute among the children. "Hey, Mrs. Jones."

"Hey, yourself."

"I want you to meet my wife, Marissa. Honey, this is Sarah, an old friend from school."

"Friend?" Sarah's brows shot skyward.

Gabe laughed. "Sarah's one of the reasons Mrs. G had me standing in the play yard corner so much."

"Punishment he surely deserved," confided Sarah, a tall, slim woman with sparkling green eyes. "Considering he wouldn't leave my pigtails alone." She swept her heavy chestnut braid over her shoulder and pretended to shudder.

The three of them laughed.

"Sarah and I have already met," she informed Gabe.

"So you know she owns the best bookstore in Dillon?"

Sarah rolled her eyes. "Gabe, it's the *only* bookstore in Dillon. That being said—" she turned to Marissa "—you're welcome to stop in anytime. No need to buy—just come visit."

"Thank you. I'd like that."

"Same goes for me." At the sound of the deep voice from behind her, Marissa turned. Approaching her was the sandy-haired man she had noticed earlier, whose head and shoulders towered above everyone else in the room.

"Tanner Jones," Gabe put in. "My wife, Marissa. Honey, this is the lucky guy who got Sarah. But I wouldn't recommend visiting his place of business. He's the local deputy sheriff."

She smiled. "That must make your place the town jail?"

"Sure does." Tanner reached to shake her hand.

"Thank you for the invitation, Deputy Jones, though I believe I might find the bookstore more welcoming."

"I think you're right there," Sarah said.

Tanner laughed and touched a stray curl that had escaped Sarah's braid. She looked up, giving him a brilliant smile.

Marissa couldn't keep from wondering if Gabe would ever touch her so gently, so tenderly again—when it wasn't just playacting.

After a few minutes of conversation, Sarah and her husband slipped away. Gabe put his arm around her shoulders.

And now she couldn't suppress the shiver of pure desire that shot through her. Mortified by her instinctive response to him, she clenched her teeth but managed to force her lips into a smile.

"Uh-uh, Marissa. Not very natural. Looks like you just backed into a prickly pear."

He slipped his arm to her waist. Even above the loud conversations and laughter flowing around them, she could hear her breath catch.

"C'mon, now," he murmured. "Gotta convince the neighbors, remember? Show 'em the happy bride and groom?"

"I've acted happy all evening."

"From the other side of the room. I sure can't play the smitten husband with my wife half a house away."

"I've been socializing," she pointed out. "You've been busy, too."

"I'm here now. Time to act like the perfect couple. At least we dressed for the parts." He caught her left hand and lifted it to his lips. His eyes held hers, forced her to watch him as he pressed a kiss against her wedding band.

Then he turned her hand over to kiss her palm.

Her heart gave a lurch.

Wrong. All wrong. Acting like her loving husband was just that for Gabe—an act—while she hadn't the performance skill to hide her reaction to his every glance, his every touch.

To her dismay, he wrapped his other arm around her, bringing their bodies close together.

"Hey, Miller," shouted one of the men in the crowd, "ain't your honeymoon finished yet?"

Looking over her shoulder, Gabe called back, "Heck, Charlie, it's just getting started."

"The mistletoe's that way," a woman called.

"See," he murmured in her ear, "it's working already." He released her but then took her by the elbow and moved forward.

Unless she wanted to make a scene in front of all these people she already liked and who already seemed to like her, unless she wanted to look like Mrs. Scrooge instead of Gabe's blushing bride, she had no choice but to move with him.

He stopped beneath the small green sprig dangling from the overhead light in the middle of the room. Amid laughter and loud hoots, he took her in his arms again.

She glanced up, then blurted in a whisper, "Wait. That's not mistletoe, it's holl—"

Too late. Gabe's lips had claimed hers.

As always, the chemistry sparked between them, as bright and shiny as the flashing twinklers on the Christmas tree. The attraction was too strong to fight, too overwhelming to ignore. Too good to miss. So she didn't.

She accepted Gabe's lingering kiss. Matched him move for tantalizing move.

And gave a darned good show for the cheering crowd.

"WELL, IF THAT lip-lock didn't beat all," Delia Brand said as Doc walked into his kitchen, "I don't know what would."

"That was a wonderful idea of yours, Delia, mentioning the mistletoe. Still…" Lily frowned. "Though they did a superb job of trying to hide it, I suspect trouble."

"Sure enough," Delia said. "They spent half the night circling each other like a pair of tomcats spoiling for a fight."

"Do you think anyone else noticed?"

"Nah. They were too busy lining up to meet Marissa."

"We've got to do something to help."

"Why'd you think I said that about the mistletoe?" Delia chuckled. "Gabe sure took up the idea pretty quick."

"That boy needs someone in his life. He needs Marissa. And now that she's back, we've got to make sure she stays—"

"Whoa, Nellie," Doc interrupted. "You women can't go sticking your noses into Gabe's private business."

Delia shook with laughter. "Private? In Dillon? Doc, you know better than that. People have got about as much privacy around here as the desserts in my front display case."

He had to admit you couldn't miss the sweets as soon as you walked into Delia's Diner.

"Dessert!" Lily Gannett cried, eyes gleaming behind her glasses. She pushed a plate of leftovers aside and put her palms flat on the counter. "That's it, Delia."

He didn't need his medical degree to diagnose the signs. Lily had found a new cause.

She lived to run things. School-board meetings. Picnics. The annual Founder's Day festival. Other people's lives.

If she'd decided to focus her talents on Gabe and Marissa, those two didn't stand a chance.

"We can take care of Marissa," Lily said. "Everyone just raved about her dishes and desserts and homemade candy. I told her the women would be lining up for recipes."

"Heck, I wouldn't mind some of them myself. Or, even better, maybe I can rope her into baking for the diner. We could use a few new selections during the holiday season."

"Just what I was thinking!"

Doc had to admit it was a good idea. Marissa sure could cook.

"All right, Delia. You speak to her about doing some orders for you. I'll get a few women together. Doc, what about you?"

His smile faded. "Hold on. I'm not involving myself—"

"Now, Doc," Lily said, and he recognized the schoolteacher tone right off, "don't act like this is the first time we've taken a hand in bringing two people together. See how well Sarah and Tanner are doing."

He nodded his agreement.

"We've known Gabe all his life," she continued, "and a hard time he's had of it, too. He finally has a chance for lasting happiness. How will you feel if Marissa leaves town again, and you haven't done anything to help him keep her here?"

"That still doesn't give me the right to go interfering—"

"Doc," Delia cut in, "you helped birth that boy."

"She's right. That certainly allows you to concern yourself with his welfare." Lily's normally sweet expression had disappeared, replaced by a commanding frown.

Delia, sturdy arms crossed, looked twice as unyielding.

"In fact, Doc," Lily added, "close as you've been to him his whole life, you owe it to him."

He sighed.

In all seriousness, that night he'd told Gabe the truth: he'd spent a lifetime taking care of this town. And Gabe himself had razzed him about handing out advice left and right. Guess that could include some marriage counseling.

"All right," he said. "I reckon I can take an interest."

LATE THE NEXT MORNING, Gabe kicked his heels up onto the coffee table in front of the couch and couldn't hold back a grin.

Holding and kissing Marissa had added a real perk to this pretend marriage. She'd liked it, too, judging by the way she'd responded. Soon as he could, he intended to kiss her again. They needed to get back in practice.

He'd come to that decision last night, same time he'd decided he'd been riding the right path all along. Keep Marissa on the ranch. Wait in due course till she delivered the baby, if there was one. Then get Doc to run whatever tests necessary to prove whether or not he'd fathered the child.

The telephone on the side table rang. Before he could grab it, Marissa answered the extension in the kitchen. Her voice drew him to his feet.

When he entered the room, she had already hung up the phone and stood filling a roasting pan. Only an hour till Sunday dinner, and the smell of something tasty permeated the air.

She looked tasty, too, in a pale blue sweater and white denim jeans, her hair piled up and twisted into a knot on top of her head. He couldn't resist coming up behind her and dropping a kiss on the back of her bare neck.

Her grip on the pan tightened. Months before, she'd

have turned around so he could kiss her properly. Yeah, she'd sure lost the habit.

"Short conversation," he said. "Wrong number?"

"No, it was Doc."

"I was only in the other room. Why didn't you holler?"

"He called to talk to me."

He raised his brows. "I knew Doc liked you, but calling another man's wife seems pushy, don't you think?"

"Don't be ridiculous. I told him I need his professional services, and he checked his appointment book for me this morning. He's penciled me in for tomorrow."

Frowning, he took her by the hand.

"An appointment with Doc? What for? Something wrong with the baby?" For a moment, all his doubts had fled. The skin around her eyes puckered as if she felt pain, and his heart thudded. "What is it, sweetheart?"

"Nothing." She sidled out from between him and the counter, pulling her hand from his. "There's nothing wrong. I like Doc and I'm due for a regular checkup and I decided to make the appointment with him."

"He knows you're pregnant?"

"He will tomorrow."

He considered, then nodded. "Good. Once Doc finds out, no reason the whole town can't hear about the baby, too."

She stiffened. "Let's give it a little while longer."

Long enough for her to pack up and leave town?

The thought struck him hard. All along, he'd focused on keeping her there, finding out what motives she had for coming back, seeing if she really was carrying his child. His plan kept him from facing the fear that she might leave, no matter what he did to keep her.

"I'll start to show soon," she added, "and everyone will know then anyway."

"Even more reason to act like a happily married couple." He reached for her again. She stepped back.

"C'mon, Marissa. We need the practice."

"We certainly do not. And I don't think we need to 'practice' in public at all. You didn't see any other man drag his wife under that so-called mistletoe last night, did you?"

"Yeah, but we're newlyweds."

"Not good enough, as you're so fond of saying. I'm not so sure this pretend marriage is necessary, except for offering you some fringe benefits you seem all too ready to take advantage of."

He winced, recalling his thoughts about the perks of holding and kissing her.

"But," she finished, planting her fists on her hips, "I don't see where this farce offers me anything in return."

"You seemed to like it well enough last night."

Sudden tears sparkled in her eyes. He started to reach for her, until she held a palm out to hold him off and he realized she wasn't ready to cry but to curse him.

"Kissing you was never the problem, Gabe. Neither was making love with you. You know that. Before I left, I tried telling you a marriage needed more than that. Nothing has changed. And if you think I'll stay when you're the only one to benefit from this bargain, you'd better rethink the issue."

Panic shot through him. He imagined her taking off, never to return. "We agreed."

"Yes, for the baby's sake. Only you're pushing things too far, using this pretend marriage to get what you want without giving anything back. Take that kiss at the party. I'm just not willing to playact to that extent any longer. Not without a few concessions from you."

"Like what?"

"Like…like—"

His panic trickled away. He had her. Blasting off with her crazy notions, probably not even knowing what all she'd said. Probably not meaning half of it.

"Like courting me." He heard the triumph in her tone.

He laughed incredulously. "If that isn't the most—"

"Oh, no, Gabe Miller." She moved so close he could see her hazel eyes had darkened to an ominous shade. "You're the one who claims to be so old-fashioned about everything. Well, then, courting a woman ought to be just your style."

"That's for people getting to know each other. You're already my wife."

"Maybe that's where we went wrong—skipping straight to marriage without learning much about each other first."

He frowned and crossed his arms over his chest. "You were happy enough with the idea then."

"Yes, Gabe, I admit it. But how good could the idea have been, if our marriage couldn't last even three weeks?"

"When you walked out."

"Yes, I did. After telling you over and over again how I felt. After trying so hard to get you to open up with me. Are you saying I was the only one at fault for giving up on us?"

He set his jaw.

"We didn't have a courtship then—we barely had a relationship. But I want it now. We need to take a step back and do it right this time. Think it over, cowboy."

Before he could move or speak, she turned on her heel and stomped out of the kitchen.

Damn.

Shaking his head, he grabbed a piece of raw carrot from the roasting pan and chomped a piece off it.

She was already his wife. And why should he try so hard to please her, when he couldn't trust her? Hell, he hadn't even been able to rely on her to file for the divorce.

How could he expect that she'd stay this time? She'd left once to go back to the big city. She could—and probably would—do it again. Like a few other people he could name. Folks had a habit of running out on him.

Double damn.

He tossed the remaining bit of carrot in the trash.

His head told him Marissa would only leave again. His heart said to kick her out while he was still in one piece. But his gut warned him to slow down and think things through.

If she was pregnant, if they had made a child, that baby was the only real family he had.

If she took off somewhere, he might never find her.

No way would he let that happen. Not until he'd learned the truth.

He found Marissa on the living room couch with her feet up and her arms wrapped around her knees. The position suggested she had no interest in compromise. So did the look on her face. She wouldn't turn his way, just stared across the room as if the Seth Thomas clock on the corner shelf fascinated her.

For a minute, he stood there, taken back to when they'd met, before all the trouble had started between them.

Then he hardened his heart.

"All right, Marissa. You've got a deal."

She whipped her head around to face him. Her eyes wide and locked on his, she rose from the couch.

Good.

The surprises weren't over yet. He might have to swallow his pride, accept her demand until things straightened themselves out. But that didn't mean he had to follow all the rules.

He crossed the room and stopped in front of her.

"I'll make the concessions you asked for." Keeping his touch easy, he cupped his hand under her chin. "Now, let's seal the bargain."

Chapter Seven

The next morning, the sound of Gabe's shower sent Marissa running out to the bunkhouse kitchen earlier than usual. She was determined to keep her distance from him.

By the time he arrived, smelling soap-fresh and with his hair damply curling, she was well into breakfast preparation.

She chopped ruthlessly at the green peppers on her cutting board and tried to keep from grinding her teeth.

The night before, she had felt happy when Gabe agreed to court her. His willingness seemed to show they had reached a new phase in their relationship, one that might lead them where a true marriage should go. To an emotional closeness, a bonding, that went far beyond sexual attraction.

Then he had taken her in his arms, and her untrustworthy heart had given in without the slightest resistance. For the briefest moment, she'd thought of nothing but him. Almost too late, she had come to her senses and torn herself away. How could she have let herself give in? For him, their kisses meant little beyond regaining the respect of his friends.

Worst of all was the feeling that Gabe knew exactly what his touch did to her, and exactly when to use it to his advantage.

She wouldn't—*couldn't*—let him entice her again.

She gave the final chunk of pepper a chop solid enough to make him jump.

"Feeling energetic this morning?" he asked.

"Yes."

Warren and the other men entered the room.

"Good morning," she greeted them, relieved that she was no longer alone with Gabe.

Taking advantage of the distraction, she sidled away from him. Knowing he watched made her move as stiffly as though she'd lined the floor with discarded eggshells.

Only a roomful of starving cowboys could have missed her awkward escape—and, luckily, she'd learned, Gabe's cowboys were always starving.

Unfortunately, Warren noticed more than the rest. She caught him staring at her and forced a quick smile. "Western omelets, coming right up."

"Sounds great, doesn't it, boss?"

"Yeah," Gabe muttered.

Her back to him, she braced herself for his approach. He would close the gap between them, would force her to play the loving bride in front of witnesses.

But, to her surprise, he took his seat at the table.

It wasn't until later, after the other men had left the kitchen and Gabe followed close on their heels, that she realized he hadn't had any trouble avoiding her.

This piqued her interest. Why ignore her today, when last night he'd agreed to court her?

SHORTLY AFTER NINE o'clock that morning, Marissa stood outside Delia's Diner. Through the glass door, she could see the smoky haze from frying bacon hanging in the air. The scent of it stirred the queasiness she had managed recently to hold off.

Once done with her appointment with Doc, she had driven to the diner. For the first time in weeks, she felt hungry for a full meal before noon. She'd barely gotten down a piece of toast at breakfast.

Inside, she found warmth and cheerfulness and more than a few friendly faces.

She made her way past the high counter stools, stopping here and there to return the greetings of people she'd met at Doc Thompson's party. By the time she found a vacant booth, she was blinking hard against a sudden threat of tears.

In all the places she had lived over the years, she had never met people who were this nice to her. Had her mother's behavior—her lousy taste in men and fondness for loud brawls—influenced them? Or were the citizens of Dillon just much more welcoming than the rest?

Growing up, she'd always wished for a hometown like this one, filled with people who'd known each other practically since birth and who genuinely cared about one another. Now, after one introduction at one party, this small Texas town offered her the opportunity to have that wish fulfilled.

Yet one thing stood in her way. The one person who mattered most, who could make her dream of a happy family come true.

Her husband.

With a heavy sigh, she slid into the booth and grabbed the plastic-coated menu tucked between the salt and pepper shakers.

The diner's owner approached, carrying a coffee carafe. Marissa had met her, also, at Doc's party.

"Morning, Mrs. Miller. Nice of you to happen in." Delia hoisted the carafe.

Marissa shook her head. "No, thanks. I'll have orange juice, please, and pancakes."

"Bacon or sausage on the side?"

"N-no. Just the pancakes." She stared down at the closed menu, willing her stomach to settle.

By the time breakfast arrived, she felt fine again— and suddenly ravenous. Without even waiting for Delia to depart, she dug in.

"Delicious," Marissa told her after a forkful of fluffy pancake.

"Thank you kindly. Around here, I'm known for good home cooking. Not fancy, but filling."

Marissa froze. Had that been an intended insult to her cooking? And why did she feel hurt at the idea of it?

Maybe because her cooking success was all her father found in her worthy of praise. Maybe because her skill in the kitchen was all that made her useful on Gabe's ranch.

"Wish I had your talent with the gourmet goods, though," Delia continued, "especially those fancy desserts. Any chance you'd whip me up some for the diner for the next little while?"

For a long moment, Marissa sat speechless. Guilt at her earlier suspicion made her want to cringe, while surprise and pleasure threatened to reduce her to tears again. "I would love to do some baking for you."

Delia beamed.

They arranged the business details and shook hands—very different from the way Gabe had insisted on settling *their* deal.

Marissa pushed the thought away, then watched as Delia headed back toward the counter. To her amusement, Delia gave a thumbs-up and hissed a long, drawn-out, "yessss." Quite an enthusiastic reaction over an order of pastry.

Still smiling, she returned her attention to the pancakes.

A few minutes later, Sarah Jones entered the diner and headed straight to her booth. "What brings you to town this early, Marissa?"

"Breakfast, for one thing." She indicated her almost-empty plate. "Join me?"

At the party, she'd felt an immediate connection to Sarah. Yet, as much as she would love to talk about her pregnancy with the other woman, a mother herself, Marissa hesitated.

No matter how rocky their relationship, Gabe was

the father of her child. He had the right to share in the announcement about the baby on the way when—*if*— she ever felt ready to share the news. She didn't want people congratulating them, asking for updates, watching her grow, until she and Gabe were prepared for that.

She tried to focus on Sarah, who slid into the bench seat opposite her.

"I can't stay but a minute," the other woman said. "The store opens at nine-thirty." She smiled. "On my morning walk, I spotted you through the window. If you're finished and looking to while away some time, why don't you come and visit?"

"That would be nice." She left a tip and went with Sarah to the cash register.

Delia set her spatula beside the sizzling griddle and shuffled down the narrow aisle behind the front counter to take her bill. "Now, don't forget those cream puffs 'n' such for me."

"Don't worry, I won't," Marissa assured her. "I'll see you on Wednesday afternoon." She followed Sarah out to the sidewalk. "Delia hired me to make some desserts for her over the holidays," she explained.

"Delia's a shrewd businesswoman—knows a good thing when she sees it. Folks will flock into the diner when they hear the news. Maybe I ought to get you to do a few sweets for the bookstore, too, if you can handle the volume."

Marissa held back a smile, remembering the Women's Club Tea and Social—sandwiches and dessert for two hundred—that she'd prepared single-handedly a month earlier.

They passed Doc Thompson's house with its first-floor office, then a pharmacy and several other storefronts.

"Not much to Main Street," Sarah said. "The town of Dillon itself isn't large. Most of the acreage sprawls outside the town proper into ranch land."

Marissa glanced down the length of the commercial section. Just a few blocks long, it took up less space than the property of her father's Chicago hotel.

"How do you manage to run a—?" She stopped, warmth tingling her cold cheeks. "I'm sorry, that's none of my business."

Sarah laughed. "You must not come from a small town or you'd know everything that goes on is *everyone's* business. And it's a darn good question. Fortunately, sales pick up for me in the wintertime. When there's not much else to do, books are always there for people, especially the older folks. Most of the younger ones aren't big readers, not when they're working most daylight hours."

"Like Gabe." She thought of the magazines in his living room, all related to ranching and farming.

Sarah nodded.

Granted, he spent more time with her now, but three months ago he had seemed driven to work on the ranch as soon as they returned to it the week after their impromptu Las Vegas wedding.

Still, that hadn't excused him from cutting himself off from her, from communicating only once a day and in only one way. In that king-size bed with the feather mattress and cozy quilt.

In Las Vegas, at first meeting, Gabe had seemed so different. Yes, as typical newlyweds and new lovers, they could barely keep their hands off each other. Could hardly find time to speak. But when they did, Gabe had seemed so willing, so interested. He'd listened to her. He'd loved her.

Yet again, she realized how wrong she had been about that.

Because they had come to the ranch and everything had changed.

Their lovemaking had continued, between bouts of separation and silence. But it was emotional closeness they lacked.

"There it is," Sarah announced, startling Marissa from her thoughts.

She pointed to a three-story frame house painted buttercup-yellow with green shutters and white trim. The business took up the lower level, Sarah told her, with living quarters above.

The wooden sign hanging from a post set into the narrow front yard proclaimed it The Book Cellar.

"Home sweet home," Sarah said.

They went down slate steps to the glass-front door flanked by picture windows.

Inside, floor-to-ceiling bookcases lined each of the side walls. Tall wooden cases also took up most of the floor space in the front half of the store.

Sarah led her down the center aisle and past a cozy

collection of overstuffed chairs and mismatched end tables. Behind a waist-high counter draped with Christmas garland, a doorway opened into an office.

When they entered it, Sarah indicated a wooden rocker with paisley cushions for Marissa and took the swivel chair in front of a large oak desk for herself.

"Gabe's a hard worker." Sarah picked up their conversation from where they had left it before the bookstore tour.

Marissa wavered, caught between discussing her private life with a near-stranger and longing to know more about the man she had married. But she felt comfortable with Sarah, who had grown up with Gabe.

"He works too hard, I think," Marissa offered.

"That's natural when you love the land. And he does, same as his daddy and granddaddy. They raised Gabe alone on that ranch since before he was the age of my Kevin. But you know that."

Marissa shook her head. "Gabe told me both his parents were gone," she said quietly. "But he hadn't explained that he'd lost his mother so young."

No wonder he'd been so adamant about raising a child in a two-parent household. Why couldn't he just have told her his reasons?

She stared down at her hands, where her fingers twisted in her lap. "We've been married such a short time. There's so much about Gabe that I don't know." That he refused to share.

"Sometimes," Sarah said, "you can think you know a person, and life still throws you some surprises. Like reading a good book, where you never can figure what'll happen next. Trust me, Marissa. I know. Tanner and I grew up together, but we still had a lot to learn about each other. And we weren't even married yet when Gabe brought you home as his bride."

Marissa looked up in surprise.

Sarah nodded. "It's a long story, a lot of it sad. But I'll tell you some other time. Right now, you've got your own troubles. As for Gabe," she continued, "he's not used to having a woman in his life. Or…a baby."

Marissa froze. "Doc told—?" Her words froze, too, as she saw the gentle understanding in Sarah's expression.

"No, nothing to do with Doc. Or anyone else. I just took a wild guess."

"But I'm not showing at all. I'm not even due for another six months."

Sarah eyed her midsection. "You're carrying small, like I did. I doubt you'll even show till six."

"Then how could you possibly have known?"

"Honestly?" Her face lit with a sudden grin. "I saw your breakfast plate at Delia's."

Marissa stared. Then, unable to help herself, she laughed. Indignation turned to relief that her privacy hadn't been violated—and that she could trust her instincts about Sarah.

"What?" she asked. "Doesn't everyone put mustard on their pancakes?"

Sarah laughed. "Oh, I could go on and on about what I craved when I carried Kevin." Serious again, she leaned forward and spoke very softly. "That's why you came back to Dillon, isn't it?"

"Yes."

"Gabe knows about the baby?"

Marissa nodded, a lump catching in her throat.

"He's a good man, Marissa. Maybe not easy to know, surely not easy to live with. But raising a baby alone's not easy. Believe me. Work things out with each other, if you can."

Could they?

Would they ever find their happy ending, as Sarah and Tanner so obviously had?

Tears rose to her eyes. She blinked them away.

When she had first come to live on the ranch, she had failed to reach Gabe. And he had neglected to reach out to her.

What hope did she have that they could solve their problems now, when it seemed nothing had changed?

Chapter Eight

Courting his own wife.

Gabe grimaced as he stomped into Delia's. All day, the idea had run wild in his head but he still couldn't get it roped and tied. Why should a man have to put himself through that when he was already married?

He couldn't work worth a damn, either, and finally he gave in to the feeling he ought to talk things over with Doc. Warren was his oldest friend, but Doc'd always been the one he'd taken his troubles to when he didn't want them known on the ranch.

The cowhands had been surprised, but certainly not sorry, considering his mood, when he'd announced he had to head into Dillon for supplies. He hadn't even stopped by the house, just went straight into town.

At this hour, too early for supper, the diner held only an older couple sharing one of Delia's Texas-size burgers. He greeted them, then slid onto a padded stool and dropped his Stetson on the vacant seat beside him.

"What's the matter, Gabe?" Delia stared at him.

"Nothing. I want coffee."

"Uh-huh." She pulled a pot from one of the burners behind her. "I'm giving you high-test, 'cause you look like you need some get-up in you." She filled his mug to the brim. "Got some news for you."

He sipped the dark brew and waited. Delia would tell him what was on her mind in her own good time. Ought to take about three seconds.

"Your missus and me are in business."

Did it in one, and the announcement nearly caused him to spit out his mouthful of coffee. He set down his mug in a hurry.

Did this mean Marissa had decided to stay? His heart gave a funny sideways lurch. That had to be Delia's high-test, which got stronger as the day wore on.

"Talked to her this morning," she confirmed. "She's going to be doing some baking for me through the holidays."

"Oh, yeah?"

Through the holidays. So, it didn't mean anything permanent, after all. Why he'd expected more, he didn't know.

The door opened, and they both turned to look. With relief, Gabe saw Doc enter the diner.

"I'll have the usual, Delia."

That meant the high-test, double-strength, hold the sugar and cream. Doc drank more coffee than anyone in town.

"C'mon back, Doc," Gabe told him. "We need to talk."

He led the way toward Doc's regular booth in the far corner.

Gabe put his mug down, slid onto the bench, then waited as the older man settled across from him. He bided his time till Delia had delivered Doc's coffee and departed. Then he started in.

"Doc, you'll never believe this one."

"What is it, son?"

"It's Marissa, that's what. Marissa and her foolish ideas. She says we never had a regular relationship because we went and got married so fast. Never had a chance to get to know each other well enough. So she wants all that now." He shook his head. "She wants me to court her, Doc."

To his surprise, her crazy notion didn't seem to faze the other man.

Gabe tried not to growl. "It's just not natural."

Doc almost choked on his coffee.

"Well, it isn't," Gabe insisted.

"How are things going out at the ranch?"

He shrugged. "Fine."

"It's just a week now since Marissa came back, isn't it?"

That started him off again. "Yeah. Just a week since she started cooking for me and the boys and taking care of the house. And now she's starting up in business with Delia."

Doc's white eyebrows shot up. "What's this?"

Gabe explained the arrangement.

"Well, that sounds promising. And what are you doing to help the relationship?"

"Me?" Gabe glared. "Same as I did before. Same as I've always done. I work to provide for her. Guess that's not enough."

Though she did do the cooking now, his hard labor put that food on the table. And though she'd turned him down cold, he'd offered to share his bed with her. What more could he do?

Doc sighed. "I hear what you're telling me, son. But it's different for women. They like their men to show 'em how they feel. Courting is a traditional way of doing that."

Yeah. He hadn't told Doc about how, the morning she'd come back, he'd shot off his big mouth about being old-fashioned. And how she'd later used it as ammunition, a double barrel right between the eyes.

"I don't know what she's looking for." He put his head in his hands.

"It's not hard to figure, Gabe. A nice dinner out sometime. A few compliments. Some surprises. Candy, flowers, or maybe something special to her."

Gabe rolled his eyes. "Damn, Doc. Courting my own wife?"

"Gabe, Marissa seems a woman who knows her mind." Doc shook his head. "My advice, no charge today, take it or chuck it. Best think hard about what she's asking."

Gabe focused on his Stetson on the seat beside him and ran his thumb along the brim. "You saw her this morning, Doc?" he asked, voice low.

"I did." Doc's tone matched his.

"Then you know…" He swallowed hard.

"That she's pregnant."

"Is she?" He looked up now, as if not meeting his friend square in the face had made his question less straightforward. Less blunt and cold than he knew it to be. But he didn't know how else to put it.

And he had to have an answer.

Doc studied Gabe. Was he bracing himself to relate some bad news?

Gabe's fingers clamped onto the Stetson's brim.

"Now, what would cause you to ask a question like that?"

He shrugged. "Face it, Doc. She's been gone for months. How do I know she's telling the truth?"

The older man stared him down, his gray eyes as piercing as the bright penlight he used during his medical exams, revealing all Gabe's ills, as he always did. Following up with strong medicine as needed.

"You could start by trusting her."

His dry, humorless laugh made his throat ache. "Forget trust. I need facts."

Doc sighed and shook his head. "All right, then. The facts are, yes, your wife is pregnant. And the timing's right for the baby to be yours."

GABE STARED at the bunkhouse kitchen windows, where he could see Marissa fixing supper.

So she had told the truth about carrying a baby. He was going to be a father—and to him that meant also being a husband. He'd left Delia's determined to give

Doc's ideas a try, to find a way to start courting Marissa and give her reason to stick around.

On his way out of town, he'd stopped at the market.

Now, he snatched up the gift he'd bought and hustled into the main house and through the kitchen to the hall. He'd leave the flowers on the coffee table for her to find after supper. That ought...

He stumbled to a halt in the living-room doorway. His jaw dropped.

Damn. She'd beat him to it.

Pine boughs were draped around every window. Holly sprigs decorated every sill. Yellowish-colored poinsettia plants sat here and there on the floor. Bright red ones in wicker baskets nearly covered the top of the coffee table.

He backed a step out of the room and saw what he'd missed on his way in—the wreath on the hall wall and the pine garland wrapped around the stair rail.

Against all that deep, bright color, his handful of flowers looked straggly and sick.

He strode back to the kitchen and buried the tissue-wrapped package in the trash. Better to look as if he'd done nothing than to offer something so puny by comparison.

Seconds later, as he shoved a hand through his hair in frustration, the door opened and Marissa stepped inside.

"Gabe? I heard the truck. You're in early. Is every-thing all right?"

"Yeah." Still peeved at himself, he didn't want to mention going to town.

She slipped out of her coat and hung it on the peg by the door. "We'll eat at the regular time, then?"

"Yeah, the boys'll come in same as usual."

He knew she'd made them all a good meal. She'd stuck to her end of their agreement. Well, one way or another, he would come up with something to prove he was doing his part, too.

"I decorated a little today for the holidays."

"Yeah, I saw."

"Doc's house looked so nice when we were there for the party, it made me feel envious." She laughed. "I also bought a live tree at the hardware store."

He nodded. That news, added to what Delia had told him about Marissa's baking for the diner, told him she planned to stay through Christmas, at least.

Hell, that only meant another four days.

"The tree was too big for my car, so they're holding it for me. Do you think you could pick it up with the truck?"

"No problem. I'll go now. Need to get a few things, anyway." That would cover his making a trip to town today, and she'd never know about the flowers unless somebody from the market flapped their jaw.

He reached the back door before a question stopped him. So caught up in gift buying—in courting his own darned wife—he'd forgotten. "Had your appointment with Doc today?"

"Yes." She smiled. "He said everything is as it should be, and as long as I take my vitamins and feel okay, I don't need to see him again for two weeks."

"Two weeks, huh?" His eyes met hers and locked.

"That makes the appointment exactly three weeks from the day you got back here."

"Yes." She stared him down.

He'd have curried Sunrise with a toothbrush before breaking that gaze.

A few seconds later, she glanced away.

He eased over to stand beside her, kept his voice low and smooth as he said, "That's a familiar time frame, isn't it, honey?"

She stared at him again, then closed her mouth on whatever she'd planned to say and crossed her arms over her belly.

Almost against his will, his eyes dropped to her middle. He forced himself to look up again.

"Yes, it's a familiar time frame," she said finally. "Three weeks. That's the same length of time we had been married when I...left."

He had to wonder if she'd stay as long this time around. Under his jacket, he shifted his shoulders, trying to shake off the feeling of dread that had oozed into every bone in his body.

TO MARISSA'S SURPRISE, Gabe had kept his promise and gone into town for the Christmas tree she had bought. She stood at the sink, dumbfounded, as he carried the twine-wrapped bundle through the kitchen.

Her emotions topped another crest on the roller coaster she had been riding all afternoon and evening.

After an uneventful dinner in the bunkhouse, she had returned alone to the main house.

As she'd lifted the kitchen's waste-can lid to dispose of some trash, she'd spotted an edge of green tissue paper wrapped around a bunch of pale-yellow and white chrysanthemums.

Flowers.

Stunned, she'd dropped onto the nearest chair. Her heart seemed to swell.

Gabe was courting her. Because she had demanded it? Or because he really wanted to? And why hadn't he given them to her?

Her mind worked crazily, spinning fantasies about what this might mean.

Of course! He had seen all the decorating she had done and, for some reason, felt his flowers didn't measure up. How touching. And how wonderful that he had tried, at least, to make her happy.

She wouldn't embarrass him by letting on that she knew what he had done. She understood trying to impress someone and not meeting standards.

Finally coming back to the moment, she hurried down the hall in anticipation of what would happen next between them.

Keeping her distance protected her from the danger of giving in to his advances. But constant avoidance would only prevent them from ever solving their problems and reaching a happy ending.

She was determined to have Gabe spend time with her. If he would listen as she told him how she felt, if he could understand and relate to what she said, maybe he would open up and share his own thoughts with her.

He had strong feelings; she knew it. She had seen the emotion in his eyes that afternoon, before he'd turned and left the kitchen.

Maybe a few relaxing hours together, without any of the cowboys around, would do the trick.

After all, they should be celebrating the good report of her doctor visit. Instead, they had let it cause conflict between them. They should be sharing the thrill of their baby-to-be. Instead, Gabe had focused on a part of their history she didn't want to relive.

Yet he had attempted to court her.

And now, she found, as she entered the living room, he was setting up the Christmas tree for her.

She went to the couch and shifted aside the bags of ornaments she had placed there earlier. She glanced at the pine boughs and holly and poinsettias, and felt a touch of satisfaction. She had put her stamp on the room, made it feel partly hers, which made her feel more at home and welcome.

So did Gabe's intention to court her.

But when he had finished making sure the tree stood straight and secure, he turned away.

Her heart sank. He couldn't talk if they spent the evening apart. Or, worse, in separate houses.

"Aren't you staying? I thought we might do this as a team."

He shrugged, not meeting her eyes. "I haven't decorated a tree in years."

"I can beat that. I've never decorated a tree in my life."

His gaze flew to hers. "Never?"

She shook her head. Holding her breath, she began taking out ornaments and setting them on the couch.

To her relief, he reached into one of the bags for a string of lights and began unwinding them from their cardboard holder.

"So, how come you never had a tree?"

She winced, sorry now she'd blurted out that information, knowing what painful issues it would raise. But shc'd been desperate. She needed him to stay.

"I didn't say I never had one, just that I'd never decorated one."

"How come?" he asked again. He began weaving the lights around upper branches.

"When I was younger, I lived with my mother. She didn't like live trees. And we moved so much, she didn't want to cart an artificial one around with us."

No Christmas trees, no dollhouses, no bicycles. Nothing to slow them down when she had a fight with the latest boyfriend and decided it was time to move on.

"That's rough."

The sympathy in his voice surprised her. It gave her hope that he might take a first step. Gave her courage to go on.

"Yes, it was rough," she agreed. "Then, I moved in with my father. He always hires an interior designer to come in to decorate his house for the holidays."

"He wouldn't let you help?"

"No. I wouldn't have done things the right way. His way." To her dismay, her voice wobbled.

Gabe must have picked up on it because he grew still.

When he spoke again, he said just the words she didn't want to hear.

"What did he think about how we got married? It wasn't done the right way. Wasn't the usual courtship—as you made sure to remind me. How does he feel about the baby?"

She tightened her grip on a loop of shiny gold garland. "He doesn't know."

"About the baby?"

"About the baby, our marriage, quitting my job."

"You didn't bother to tell him?"

She frowned. "It's not a case of bothering. It's a matter of figuring out how."

"So you're worried about him? Worried how he's going to react to the news?"

Reluctantly, she said, "It concerns me, yes."

"And your mother?"

"That doesn't worry me at all. We haven't talked since I moved in with my father."

"Whoa. Hold on here." He held out a hand and began counting off, turning down a finger at a time. "Your mother doesn't care. Your father won't like it that you haven't done things right. You haven't got any brothers and sisters—you told me that before. You haven't got a job. And you're carrying my baby." He glared at his hand, now closed into a fist, then raised his eyes to her. "Seems to me like you need a place to raise our child—permanently."

"No," she burst out. Then she lowered her voice and said, "I've told you before, Gabe. I'll give our relationship a chance. That's all I promised."

"Not good enough, Marissa."

"I'm tired of hearing that." She dropped the garland onto the couch and stood. "You sound like my father, always insisting that things be perfect. *Your* way. But I'm not buying that."

Her anger suddenly spent, she shook her head and sighed. "I tried to tell you when I was here before, Gabe. I told you again in the note I left. Things don't have to be perfect. They don't always have to be my way, either. But I have no intention of staying in a marriage without an equal partner."

He stared at her, his face a mask, proof of the stranglehold he kept on his feelings. Yet he couldn't hide the emotions that flickered, one after another, through his eyes.

See, Gabe, you do *care.*

Then why couldn't he say so? Her pulse pounded in time with the clock in the corner. Her head swam. Her stomach heaved.

Afraid she would faint or, worse, throw up on his cowboy boots, she sank to the edge of the couch. And watched in fury mixed with despair when he walked across the room without a backward glance.

And without uttering a word.

Chapter Nine

Marissa's steps dragged as she crossed the yard to the bunkhouse at the usual time, well before six in the morning. She hugged her coat around her. It was colder than normal. Or maybe the cold came from the hopelessness she felt.

After storming out of the living room the night before, Gabe had kept to himself the rest of the evening, leaving her staring at the Christmas tree with its one strand of lights trailing on the carpet where he had dropped it. She had gone to bed, where she tossed and turned half the night, aching over her inability to reach him.

With a sigh, she pushed open the door to the bunkhouse kitchen. There was only one good thing about this entire rotten morning—she had felt no sign at all of the nausea that hit on a regular basis. Thanks to Sarah and her suggestion to eat a few dry crackers before stepping foot out of bed.

Though today, she would gladly have stayed there till noon.

Inside the bunkhouse, she found Warren waiting. She smiled at the older man. They had taken to sharing a pot of tea midmorning, if Gabe wasn't around, and had become friends.

As he often helped with the meals, his appearance this morning didn't completely surprise her. But generally, she arrived to an empty kitchen.

"Hello, Warren," she said. "You're here early."

Not meeting her eyes, he mumbled a greeting.

Her pulse tripped in alarm. Now that she thought about it, she hadn't heard any movement from Gabe's room that morning. Had something happened on the ranch during the night? To one of the cowboys? To any of the horses?

To Gabe?

"What is it, Warren?"

He shrugged. "Boss headed out, wanted me to tell you he raided the icebox before he left."

"Meaning he won't be here for breakfast."

"May not be here for dinner, neither."

"Oh. Well." Fighting to hide the wobble in her voice, she turned away.

She busied herself with making breakfast, managing to converse with the cowboys, see them off for the day and clean up the kitchen, all while acting as though nothing had happened.

And it was true. Nothing had happened, to anything but her relationship with Gabe. A relationship that seemed to be nonexistent.

A relationship that, such a few short months before, had been so magical…

Though her days at the Las Vegas convention had been filled with workshops, Marissa's nights had been her own. Early in the week, she had made a reservation for a show in her hotel's dinner theater. She'd stood amid a group of people waiting to pick up their tickets.

"I draw the line at Elvis impersonators."

The deep Texas drawl, the words spoken so close to her ear, seemed meant for her alone.

Right—talk about wishful thinking. She didn't know a soul in the crowd. Still, she couldn't help turning around, couldn't resist checking to see if the rest of the man lived up to his voice.

One look told her he did. One glance into a pair of light brown eyes set in a tanned face. Like dollops of rich caramel atop a creamy chocolate mousse.

She stared like a starved chocoholic.

"Impersonators?" She echoed his last word and forced her gaze to the billboard beside the theater entrance. "There aren't any in this show. Tonight's entertainment is a magician."

"I was talking about those guys in the wedding chapels who dress up like Elvis to marry people."

"And you were saying this to me?" She looked around for the woman he must have mistaken her for.

"Sure was." He readjusted his Stetson.

"I don't get the connection, unless you were propositioning me, cowboy?"

"Sure was," he repeated, with a laugh that crinkled the tanned skin around his eyes.

She laughed, too, feeling safe with so many people

within arm's reach. And willing to engage in an innocent flirtation with a handsome man. She certainly could use the practice.

"That's rushing things a bit, don't you think, considering we've never met."

"I know what I want when I see it." And then he looked her over, from head to foot.

Refusing to let his examination unsettle her, she did the same. Her gaze traveled upward from a pair of leather boots, to formfitting jeans, to a plaid Western shirt that strained against his biceps as he crossed his arms. When she reached those light brown eyes again, her insides unsettled themselves without any help from him at all.

Pull yourself together, girl. He's probably killing time until his date shows up.

Ahead of them, the theater box office opened. The crowd surged forward, eager to claim their reserved tickets.

Marissa kept waiting for the woman who would claim this cowboy.

"So," she asked, "what brings you to town?"

"Rodeo up north, then a detour here to meet a friend."

At the counter, she received her ticket, then moved aside. The cowboy gave his name as Gabe Miller.

Gabe.

Hard. Rugged. To the point. Just like the man himself.

Marissa looked at her watch. "I hope she's not late."

"He. Caught an early flight out this afternoon."

"Oh." Her heart gave an extra hard thump.

Maybe the charming Gabe Miller wasn't waiting for someone, after all. Maybe he wasn't teasing with his outrageous flirtation.

Maybe she should get her head examined.

A moment later, an usher appeared. "Are you together?"

"Sure are," Gabe announced. He tipped back his hat. The lights blazing above the theater's entrance caught him full in the face, making her heart do double time. "Right, Marissa?"

"R-right," she stuttered.

He reached for her hand and tucked it into the crook of his arm. "Let's go see some magic tricks."

As he escorted her into the theater, Marissa shook her head at her own boldness. They were in a public place. Surrounded by people. And, no matter the strength of her instant attraction to Gabe, they would go their separate ways after dinner and the show.

But the fact remained, she had just agreed to spend several hours with a complete stranger.

The usher led them to a rectangular table for eight. She sank into one of the seats closest to the stage, trying to steady everything that had been thrown into a kaleidoscopic whirl—the room, her pulse, her heart.

As Gabe settled beside her, resting his arm on the back of her chair, she noted his aftershave, a subtle woodsy scent that made her unsteadier yet.

They still had to wait for the house lights to dim, for the curtain to rise, for the entertainment to start.

But for Marissa, the magic had already begun—

In the bunkhouse kitchen, the telephone rang, its loud jangle yanking her from that magical past and dropping her, with a bone-jarring thud, into her unhappy present.

LATER THAT DAY, Marissa tried to keep her mind on the activity in the ranch-house kitchen.

After suffering through breakfast without Gabe, she had been surprised to hear Mrs. Gannett's voice on the phone. Gabe's ex-schoolteacher had called as spokesperson for a group of the local wives, who wanted a lesson in candy making. Needing a diversion from her misery, Marissa had invited them for that afternoon.

To her delight, she found the day to be one of the happiest she had ever spent on the ranch. Or it would have been, if not for her constant thoughts about the trouble with Gabe.

The kitchen door swung open, and Warren came in. "Just lookin' for a cake of soap for the bunkhouse kitchen."

Marissa couldn't help chuckling, knowing she had put several unwrapped bars under the sink the day before. The women insisted he try one of their handmade chocolates. He ate several.

"All right, that's enough, Warren," she said, feeling comfortable with teasing him. "You'll spoil your dinner."

"No way, missus." He grinned. "You know my appetite won't quit when you're serving supper."

"Even so. You need to leave these ladies some candy to take home to their families."

He pretended hurt. "Reckon I'll just head out to the barn, then. Better save some for Gabe when he gets back from town, else he'll pitch a fit he missed out."

Marissa grabbed a package of soap from beneath the sink and followed him out to the porch. "Forgetting something, Warren?"

He shrugged sheepishly. "Guess we're not needing that yet, after all."

"I didn't think so, you scoundrel." She smiled, paused and took a deep breath. Trying to sound casual, she said, "Gabe's not back yet by any chance, is he?"

"He came back in the middle of the afternoon but headed right out again."

"Did he say anything special when you saw him?"

"Nope. The boss ain't one for talking much. And he'd have my hide for tellin' you this, but the boys and I ain't the only ones who think it's good to have you back, Marissa."

"R-really?" Her voice broke. She blinked away a rush of tears. Sarah yesterday, Warren today, both reassuring her.

She appreciated their help. But it wasn't they who should be trying to make her feel at home.

Warren cleared his throat. "So don't you worry about him not stopping by." He lowered his voice. "Probably saw Lily Gannett's car and knew if he went inside, for sure he'd never make it back to town before the stores closed down. That woman could talk the shine off a spanking new saddle."

She laughed, certain he had meant to cheer her.

"Thank you, Warren. I'll make sure to save some extra candy for you."

Slowly, she retraced her steps to the kitchen, where she spent the rest of the afternoon, between candy lessons, wondering why Gabe had gone to town and when he would be back.

And why, if he was so gosh-darned happy she had returned to Dillon, he refused to tell her himself.

As MARISSA HELPED her guests pack fresh chocolates between layers of waxed paper, the familiar rumble of Gabe's pickup truck shattered her concentration. The engine noise cut off, a door slammed, and footsteps struck hard against gravel.

At the sound of boots on the back porch, her heartbeat quickened, partly from tension at the memory of their last meeting and partly from an unbearable longing.

She clutched a tin of candy with suddenly shaking fingers.

The back door opened. Gabe stood in the doorway, his Stetson in one hand, a blue-and-white-striped paper sack with the pharmacy name on it in the other.

When he caught sight of the women at the kitchen table, his brow furrowed and his mouth turned down. Before anyone looked up, he was hooking his hat and jacket over their usual pegs. By the time he faced them again, the angry expression had smoothed out, leaving him with a welcoming smile.

"Afternoon, ladies." He moved to the corner of the

kitchen and shoved the pharmacy sack into the trash basket. "Looks like a chocolate factory in here."

"Marissa was kind enough to give us lessons in candy making," Mrs. Gannett told him. "But she made sure to put some aside for you."

"Did she now? That's nice of you, honey." He moved to Marissa's side, his back to the other women, his soft tone contrasting with his hard-as-steel gaze.

"Is everything okay? Warren said you'd gone into town."

"Fine."

Swallowing a sigh, she turned away from him. He had spoken in the same soft tone for the benefit of the women. His short response, though, had nothing to do with their audience and everything to do with the relationship they didn't have.

She grabbed a kitchen sponge and began swiping at the rinsed dishes in the sink. Needing something, anything, to distract her from the fact that he stood a mere foot away.

When he wrapped his warm hand around the back of her neck, a feeling of pure pleasure flowed through her. She willed herself not to allow a visible reaction to his touch.

An impossible task, considering her entire body now felt like a mound of whipped cream.

"Gabe," she muttered, keeping her voice low, mindful of the women gathered around the kitchen table. To her dismay, the warning sounded more like a plea.

She risked a glance at him. He stood grinning at her.

Smug. Satisfied. And sexier than a man had any right to be. He shifted his fingers, teasing the sensitive skin of her throat. A small, simple gesture their guests wouldn't notice or wouldn't think twice about if they had. But Gabe would know from past experience what his touch there would do to her.

She squeezed the sponge in her hand so abruptly soapy water sprayed across the counter. Cringing, she looked over her shoulder. Sure enough, the women were busy layering candy into containers. Not one of them paid any attention.

Gabe leaned next to her against the sink and crossed his arms over his chest.

Mission accomplished.

Chapter Ten

Marissa gritted her teeth and wiped up the soapy spill. She watched as Gabe teased the other women, helped them gather their candy and assisted them with their coats.

As they departed, Mrs. Gannett approached Marissa and took her hand. "Thank you again, my dear. I can't tell you what a delightful afternoon this has been. And how timely, to have all this homemade candy with Christmas just three days away." She beckoned to Gabe. When he crossed the room to stand beside them, she rested her hand on his arm. "Now, I want you both to join me for Christmas dinner."

Marissa's heart leaped at the invitation. She might have to put up a good front for their hostess, but at least she wouldn't have to worry about being alone with Gabe.

She saw a frown wrinkling his forehead. He masked it quickly behind a smile that crinkled the skin around his eyes. "Well, I don't know, Mrs. G. Some of my boys are sticking around for Christmas. Marissa might have plans for a big spread for them—"

"I'm sure they'll understand if she serves their Christmas meal at midday. I'm not planning dinner till three."

"But my bride and I might want some time alone. Still newlyweds, you know."

Her heart sank again. A whole afternoon and evening with Gabe?

Would he spend the entire time in another room, as he had the night before? Or, worse, would he while away the hours trying to seduce her, while she attempted to fight his advances?

Hardly likely she would succeed at that, when she couldn't find the will to resist him today, among a roomful of witnesses. Maybe a formal meal at Mrs. Gannett's house would keep him on his best behavior.

And keep *her* from giving in to a desire that would only lead her deeper into trouble.

"Yes," she blurted, "we'd love to have Christmas dinner with you. Thanks so much for asking."

Gabe stared at her as she tried to concentrate on Mrs. Gannett's words.

"Doc will be there, too. Tanner Jones has duty then, but Sarah and Kevin plan to join us. We'll have a lovely day." Mrs. Gannett beamed. "Well, now that's settled, I must get those ladies outside back to their homes." She nodded at Gabe. "We'll see you on Christmas, then."

Gabe grinned and held up his hands in mock surrender. "Yes, ma'am. We'll be there."

Marissa picked up Mrs. Gannett's bag of candy. As she followed the older woman across the room, she glanced over her shoulder. "I'll be right in, Gabe."

He refused to look up at her. He stood leaning against the sink again, hands on his hips, brows knitted. His bottom lip jutted out, full and sexy and—as she didn't need reminding—a perfect match for hers.

The thought sent her scurrying into her coat and through the door while she still had some of her pride intact.

Outside, she drew a deep breath of cold air and hoped it would cool her overheated body. She stood, barely conscious of Mrs. Gannett's chatter but supremely grateful for the excuse to put off her return to the kitchen.

To Gabe.

Thank goodness for the invitation to dinner. Now, all she had to worry about was getting through Christmas Eve.

Then again, he hadn't said anything about taking the day off. More than likely, it would be business as usual and, like last night, he would spend his evening with Warren and the boys.

That was all right with her.

She waved goodbye to her guests, then squared her shoulders and faced the house, knowing she couldn't put off the inevitable.

But when she walked in, her nerves strung tight in trepidation, she found the room empty, Gabe nowhere in sight.

Good. With any luck, she could finish cleaning up in here, go over to the bunkhouse and start dinner, all without crossing paths with him.

She crumpled several stray pieces of waxed paper into balls and went to throw them away. The blue-and-white pharmacy sack sat in the trash basket, right where Gabe had tossed it. The top of the bag had unfurled, giving her a view of its contents.

"What in the world—?"

She stared down at the edge of a gold foil box covered with cellophane and tied with a red velvet ribbon.

Two gifts in the trash in two days. Her heart throbbed with secret delight. And with renewed sympathy.

"Gabe," she called.

"Yeah?"

She followed his voice into the living room. He was sitting on the couch, a magazine spread across his lap. She had the distinct feeling he hadn't been reading it.

"I wanted to talk with you."

"About what?"

"About a couple of mysterious packages that have appeared in the kitchen lately."

He scowled and snapped the magazine closed. "Forget 'em."

"I can't, Gabe. I know you bought the flowers and chocolates for me. Then you saw the Christmas decorations yesterday, all the candy in the kitchen today. And you thought your gifts didn't measure up."

"Dead wrong."

Of course. She was talking about feelings, emotions. And, as always, he was shutting her out. She had to break through to him. "Gabe, you know that's not true—"

"Wrong again." He glared at her, his jaw hard. "I just changed my mind about giving 'em to you."

What could she say to that?

She simply stood there, stung speechless and stunned by the two sides of this man.

At times, he treated her so sweetly, so gently.

Yet, at other times, he seemed to wish she didn't exist.

THE NEXT AFTERNOON, Gabe walked up the back porch steps.

This…this situation between him and Marissa had damn near driven him to distraction. Here again, he'd come in early, feeling guilty for running back to the house with chores still waiting to be done. Of course, he trusted Jared and the rest to handle things on their own.

It would be nice to have the same trust in his wife.

Would he find her inside the house when he got there?

Did he even care?

He could still hear her words of yesterday, telling him what he felt. What he thought. What he meant by buying those gifts.

No way in hell would he let on to her how near to the truth she'd hit.

He'd come home carrying that five-pound box of the fanciest imported chocolates Dillon Pharmacy could provide to find his kitchen full of candy! His offering, just like the flowers the day before, had seemed down-right puny by comparison.

He yanked the back door open and stepped inside, then swore under his breath.

The room looked like a damned food factory again. From one end of the kitchen to the other, every horizontal plane was covered with desserts looking soft and sweet and tasty.

Kind of like his wife.

Ha.

She had a nerve, spouting that "equal partner" lecture at him a couple days ago. Hell, she hadn't been the only person listening to the preacher at that wedding ceremony in Vegas. He knew what being partners meant. Two people sharing things. Good times and bad. Sickness and health.

And—damn it—a marriage bed.

The way she acted, shying away every time he came near, they might never have signed that contract. No wonder he'd started feeling bitter. The injustice of it all was driving him crazy.

The courting crap only made it worse. He wanted to cut to the chase, bring her to his bedroom and get their relationship back where it belonged.

He'd taken enough chances with so-called romance. He had given Marissa his heart, only to have her return it on one of her fancy silver platters. He wouldn't try that again.

But he wasn't going to live the rest of his life without sex, either.

He was a married man, and he had the right to expect her to act like a genuine wife. After all, she was the mother of his child.

At the thought, dark suspicions rolled over him. From somewhere deep inside, he found the will to push them away.

The woman herself walked into the room, then stopped short in obvious surprise.

"Gabe. I didn't expect to see you here."

"I live here."

"I know that." Her eyes narrowed. "But you don't often show up in the middle of the afternoon."

"Where are you going?" he countered, nodding at the pocketbook she dangled from one arm.

"To Delia's, once I get these cream puffs boxed up."

"I'll go with you. It'll be a good time to announce the news."

She looked puzzled. "About what?"

"The baby."

"Oh." She swung her arms across her, covering her belly with the pocketbook, and knitted her fingers together across it.

She appeared to be protecting the baby—from him. The thought stabbed into his gut.

"Gabe, let's wait—"

"Why?"

"It's just…it's early yet."

Her pleading look sent another pain through him, and he lashed out to force it away. Same as he'd lashed out yesterday. "When's a good time, then? After you're gone?"

"That's possible."

His heart thumped double hard.

Her eyes glistened for a moment, but she blinked the moisture away. "And that's just why I don't want to tell anyone yet. Not until we've worked things out between us."

She turned on her heel and left the room.

The thought occurred to him to follow her. He reined it in.

Work things out, she'd said.

Like what? Divorce papers and visitation schedules?

CHRISTMAS EVE. Gabe shook his head and stared at the bright flowers on the coffee table, wishing the boys hadn't headed out early that afternoon. Not one of them, not even Warren, wanted to miss the potluck and poker at Charlie's place.

Gabe had refused to go along. Then he'd had to suffer through the hinting he'd have better luck at home. Ha.

Not much cause for celebrating, anyhow, when a man's starting to look like a donkey's back end.

Marissa had stuck to her part of the deal the past few days, all right, acting the perfect wife with the neighboring women. Making a special dinner for his men. Hell, even causing a near stampede at Delia's with the delivery of her baked goods yesterday—as Doc had been all too eager to relate to him that morning.

He hadn't gone to town with her after all, once she'd refused to announce the baby on the way.

And he still hadn't come up with anything to court her with. The failure had him frustrated beyond measure.

After all, a man had his pride.

He had to give her something worthy enough. Something lasting. Something that would make her want to stay on the ranch. He nearly choked on his next breath. For the first time, it had hit him.

He'd had the thought, once before, that she'd been trying to win over his men, wanting to stay on the ranch. But did her plans go beyond that?

Had she come back to get hold of his land?

He leaned his elbows on his knees, dropped his head into his upraised hand and thought furiously.

No, that didn't make sense. She'd come back to let him know about the baby. Or so she'd said. She hadn't filed for divorce. Again, or so she'd said.

In her defense, and much as he hated to support her, he couldn't recall one word she'd ever uttered that could give him the idea she wanted to take his ranch.

He breathed deeply, steadily, and the choking sensation eased.

The land had been in his family for four generations, long before he'd met her. And since she'd taken off, the ranch had returned to being all the family he had.

He hadn't thought about the property when he'd taunted her about running away, when he'd told her they should raise the child together. He hadn't realized the significance. Hadn't recognized the most important reason for keeping his eye on her. For keeping her around. Till now.

His only kin ought to be born and bred on this land, just like Gabe and the generations before him.

He had to make sure his child would inherit the ranch.

Marissa's eagerness to accept Mrs. G's invitation for tomorrow showed him how much she shied away from the idea of getting caught alone with him. Seemed like her leaving would solve that problem permanently. He couldn't risk her taking off with the baby.

Time to think seriously about hedging his bets.

He looked around at the bare tree in the corner, at the boxes of ornaments piled on the couch and across the floor.

"Hey, Marissa!"

"Just a minute," she called from the kitchen.

He crossed to the couch and waited. A moment later, she appeared in the doorway. She looked classy, elegant even, in a dark-blue sweater and tan corduroy jeans. Pure city-girl sophistication.

He shoved the thought away and concentrated on other things.

"Come sit a minute." He patted the cushion beside him.

Her eyes narrowed. "Why?"

"I want to talk to you, that's all."

She inched across the room and took a seat on the couch, leaning up against the padded arm, as far from him as she could get and still be sitting on the same piece of furniture.

Her forehead wrinkled in a frown, and her lips tightened into a pressed-down line. She didn't trust him not to touch her.

Hell, he didn't blame her.

This close, he could see lamplight reflected in her eyes and smell her shampoo. He could barely keep himself from…

He swallowed a frustrated sigh.

"Hands off tonight, Marissa."

Her lips twisted. One brow rose.

Nope. She didn't trust him by a country mile. He held up his right hand, palm out. "I promise you."

As she stared at him, the brow slowly came down again. One notch at a time, she relaxed. Her frown lines disappeared and her mouth softened. Her body shifted more comfortably against the arm of the couch.

He took a deep breath. "Listen. With Warren and the boys gone to Charlie's, we've got a long night alone ahead of us—"

Bad move. Seeing her start to tense again, he rushed on. "I'm not propositioning you, Marissa." He tried for a chuckle, but sounded choked instead. "Or maybe I am. But not the way you think. All I'm saying is, why don't we take it easy tonight. It'll be a stressful day tomorrow, playing newlyweds at Mrs. G's Christmas dinner."

"If you're not interested in accepting the invitation, I'm perfectly happy to perform without you."

"Yeah, I'll just bet." He grimaced, a heartbeat away from backing out on this crazy idea. Pride pushed him forward. He took a long deep breath and let it out slowly. "Look, I'm not saying I won't go. What I'm asking for is a truce. Why don't we just start over again, like you said the other night."

Her eyes widened. "You're serious?"

"Darn right, I'm serious."

Judging by the way her fingers twisted themselves together, she didn't entirely believe him.

"Come on," he urged, waving toward the corner of the room. "We've got a tree over there needs decorating, so why don't we begin there, see how it goes?"

"Well…I guess we could try it."

A mite begrudging, but he'd take what he could get.

"Good." He headed to the tree before she could change her mind. "I'll get going on the lights."

She moved to sit cross-legged on the floor and began threading silver hangers onto ornaments.

She focused on her work, not looking at him, but her mouth had curved upward at the corners in the sexy smile guaranteed to get him hot. His fist tightened, driving a star-shaped light into his palm. He barely noticed.

She was so damn beautiful.

And he'd promised not to touch her.

Swallowing a groan, he flopped back against the wall beside the Christmas tree. He told himself he'd fallen for a pretty face and warned himself this relationship didn't stand a chance.

None of it helped.

Oh, yeah. He'd hit it right when he said they had a long night ahead of them.

Chapter Eleven

Marissa stepped into the living room, balancing a tray holding a plate of cookies and mugs of hot chocolate. She carried it like a protective shield. She had accepted Gabe's offer of a truce, but she refused to expect anything to come of it.

She had asked him to court her, to hold off telling people about the baby. Sensitive subjects she had hoped would pierce his defensive armor. His hurtful words about each request, along with his refusal to give her the flowers and candy, made her wary of asking—or even looking—for anything more.

Gabe had moved to sit on the floor, leaning up against one end of the couch, his eyes turned to the corner of the room.

"Pretty nice, don't you think?" he asked her.

"Very nice," she answered, swallowing hard, her gaze focused on him.

He seemed mesmerized by the twinklers on the fully decorated Christmas tree. She was mesmerized by the way he looked in the reflected lights. Shadows left his eyes in darkness, but the twinklers highlighted his sturdy jawline, the slight growth of his dark beard.

Her heart ached as she stared at him. Her mind drifted to memories best forgotten.... Those hair-roughened cheeks grazing her lips. The heated firmness of his mouth against hers.

The thoughts alone sent a rush of heat through her limbs.

Gabe chose that moment to look up. She almost lost her grip on the refreshments. Hands shaking, she offered him the hot chocolate.

"Thanks." He patted the floor beside him. "Have a seat."

Relieved to sit down before she fell down, she lowered herself to the floor, setting the tray between them.

Fortunately, the refreshments proved a good distraction. He sat munching a Christmas sugar cookie. She took a tentative sip of her drink. Hot and delicious...

But not nearly as tasty as Gabe's mouth...

Cradling the mug against her raised knees, she forced herself to stare straight ahead at the Christmas tree.

They sat a long time without speaking, sharing the companionable silence. After a while, both the hot chocolate and her own raging heat mellowed to a warm glow.

She could imagine—had imagined—many nights like this one, where they would spend time together as more than lovers. As partners. Friends.

Real life hadn't happened that way. In reality, they had come nowhere near to friendship, in fact had never moved beyond the red-hot, pulse-pounding, star-struck-lovers stage. They'd spent glorious days and even more breathtaking nights together the week they were wed and on the short honeymoon that followed. No bride could have asked for a better lover. Was it wrong to crave so much more?

"I've been thinking," Gabe said, startling her.

She took a quick sip of chocolate, then cleared her throat, determined to keep her emotions from showing. "Hmm?"

"About starting over again, like we talked about."

She stiffened, not sure where this would lead. Not sure she wanted to know.

"If we did," he continued, "and we found out you were pregnant, we'd start getting ready for the baby, right?"

"It's still early," she reminded him.

"Almost four months now, Marissa. In no time at all, it'll be getting on for five. More than halfway along."

"Yes." She couldn't argue that.

"If we're in this deal to do what's best for the baby, then we've got to start thinking about him."

"Or her."

"Or her. Maybe it's too soon to start buying clothes and stuff, but it's not too soon to work on readying a place for the baby to stay."

"Stay?" She gripped the mug, trying to hold on to a whirl of emotions. Joy at his thoughts about their baby. Elation at the possibility of creating the family their child deserved.

And panic at the thought of remaining in a marriage that wouldn't fulfill her.

Not daring to breathe, she thought again about what she had said to him. About not wanting to tell anyone they had a baby on the way until they had worked things out between them.

Maybe he had realized how much she meant it.

Maybe tonight was his way of beginning.

"I haven't agreed—" she began carefully.

"Think about it," he interrupted. "Remember what you told me. About living with your mama part of your life, staying with your daddy the other. You weren't raised in a proper family."

"No. And neither were you." The words had spilled out before she could stop them.

He turned to look at her, a question in his eyes. "Picking Dillon's grapevine already, huh?"

"No, I'm not. The grapevine came to me. And I wasn't happy learning about you from someone else, instead of having you tell me directly." He didn't respond. "Anyway, no matter how I found out, I know your father and grandfather raised you."

"Yeah." He shrugged. "Wasn't so bad. They did a good job, far as I'm concerned." He leaned toward her. "You telling me that's what you want for our child?"

"Of course that's not what I want!"

Their gazes locked. Again, as once before, she could read the struggle in his eyes, could see it in his body, his stiff shoulders, clenched jaw.

She held her breath.

At last, he spoke. "The room upstairs," he said slowly. "Beside the bedroom."

"The one you use for storage?"

"Junk, mostly. I can clean it out, no problem." He shrugged. "It was my room, when I was a kid. Daddy's and Granddaddy's before me. I want to see my son—or my daughter—in it."

Not waiting for a response he thumped his mug onto the tray between them, then began gathering up the empty ornament boxes strewn on the floor beside him.

Tears clogged her throat and stung her eyes, blurring everything in the room. Gently, she placed her mug beside his. With a deep, soundless sigh, she rested her chin on her upraised knees and wrapped her arms around them, hugging them the way she wanted to hold on to her newfound hope. Gradually, she allowed herself a small, tremulous smile.

She'd long ago given up any belief in Christmas miracles. Now, maybe she ought to reconsider the possibilities.

Because just before the twinkling lights had dissolved into a tear-streaked blur, she had seen the tiniest—most resistant—most miraculous crack in Gabe's defensive armor.

GABE SURVEYED the smiling faces of the people gathered around Mrs. G's dining-room table. Mrs. G herself. Doc. Sarah Jones and her boy Kevin. And last of all, his wife.

She looked relaxed and happy, something she never

seemed to be around him. He lifted his cider glass to his mouth to hide his grimace.

"Marvelous dinner, Lily," Doc said. "Don't know when I've had a better Christmas."

Kevin looked at his mother. "Mom, what's your best Christmas ever?"

"The year Santa left you under my tree." Sarah leaned across the table to ruffle his hair.

"Aw, Mom." He ducked out from under her hand and looked at Mrs. G. "What's your best Christmas?"

"The year I got my teaching certificate."

Kevin frowned. "Why?" His brow suddenly cleared. "Oh—because that meant you didn't have to go to school anymore."

Everyone laughed.

"What about you, Gabe?" Mrs. G asked.

"Gotta be the year I got the alligator."

He saw Marissa, beside Kevin, fighting to hold back a smile.

The boy's jaw dropped. "You got an alligator for Christmas? A real one?"

"Sure enough."

"Wow! How big was it?"

"About half the size of the elephant."

"Eleph—?" He stopped. "You're fooling! Isn't he, Doc?"

Doc shrugged.

"Isn't he, Mrs. Miller?"

Gabe shifted, trying to get her to meet his gaze, but she looked only at the boy. "I don't know. You'd have to ask him," Marissa said.

Kevin turned to him again.

Gabe grinned. "Yeah, I'm fooling you, Kev."

The boy rolled his eyes and blurted, "Is it time for the presents now?"

Everyone shared a smile, including Sarah, who then shook her head and said, "Kevin! That's not polite."

"But you said after supper. And we ate."

Gabe could fully understand the youngster's confusion. He'd felt much the same way himself, after being sent in circles by the woman sitting across and down the table from him.

"First we have to do the dishes." Sarah rose, an empty plate in each hand.

Marissa followed suit, grabbing a dessert tray.

"You leave those be," Mrs. G scolded.

"Oh, no." Marissa shook her head. "After all you've done to get dinner ready, the least we can do is help clean up."

"That's right," Gabe agreed.

In the kitchen, they loaded their dishes onto the counter.

Doc gravitated toward Kevin, who had set down a plate of cookies and climbed up onto a tall stool beside it.

Out of the corner of his eye, Gabe saw Marissa slip through to the dining room again. He followed, timing his steps just right. When she leaned across the table to pick up a crumb-filled platter, he curled his hands around her hips. She started, and he heard her quick intake of breath. He smiled and wrapped both arms around her. When he nibbled at the soft skin at the back of her neck, her body trembled against him.

"Hey, honey," he whispered in her ear, "thought you could use a hand. Or two."

"This is not the place—"

"What is, then? Name it—I'll be there."

"Gabe, please."

She shifted in his arms, causing his body untold agony. He released her and stepped back before she could do any more damage.

From the kitchen, he heard laughter and a little-boy giggle.

It brought him to his senses in a way nothing else could have done at that moment.

He wouldn't risk antagonizing Marissa. Not right now, at any rate. He had to keep his end of their bargain. Keep doing what he could to court her. Then, when the worst happened and she took off, she'd have no reason to deny him contact with his child.

GABE SETTLED on Mrs. G's plushy flowered couch and balanced a mug of cider on his knee. The women had shooed the men out of the kitchen.

Sarah's son moved to the other side of the room, near the stereo currently belting out "Here Comes Santa Claus." Taking advantage of the noise, Kevin rummaged through the wrapped presents under the tree. He was a cute tyke, with his gap-toothed smile and the hank of dark hair over his forehead.

Gabe had grown up with Tanner and Sarah. A real shame, how long it'd taken them to get together, to work things out.

Would he and Marissa?

His mind couldn't finish the question.

He welcomed the distraction when Doc pushed the bentwood rocker closer to the couch and lowered himself into it. He patted his belly, covered by a red-and-white-striped vest. "Turkey and 'taters and all the trimmings. Can't beat that for a Christmas meal."

"Sure can't." Gabe forced a grin. "Cleaning off the table didn't put a dent in it. Beats me how you've got a place to put dessert."

"Always room for dessert—especially if your good woman's baking." Doc shot a glance toward the other room, then looked his way. "How's the courting going, son?"

Gabe frowned down into his cider. "Not so hot."

Irritation set in as he remembered the flowers he'd bought for nothing, the candy he'd tossed away. He shouldn't have bothered. He knew he wasn't good at this. They might've come to a temporary truce last night, might have had a fairly civil morning, but he wouldn't take bets on how long it lasted.

He felt a pang somewhere inside his chest but ignored it.

Without meaning to, he'd gotten Kevin sidetracked from his game of "best Christmas ever" before the boy could get around to asking Marissa. Didn't matter. Still, it would have been nice to hear her share a memory, even though Gabe already knew she had never had a good Christmas.

She hadn't stuck around anywhere—being on the move was part of her nature now. He couldn't trust her when he knew for certain that, sooner or later, the big city would lure her away. She'd take off, just like the first time. Deep inside, where he kept the things he didn't want to think about, he knew the relationship wouldn't work out.

Maybe a tiny part of him refused to give in. That could be why he'd mentioned to her about setting up the baby's room. But the rest of him still hedged his bets.

"Things'll turn out fine."

Gabe looked up, startled, as if Doc had read his mind.

"You get her something for Christmas?"

"You bet, Doc. All taken care of." Something else that wouldn't measure up. He forced another grin. "Planning a private party for later this evening."

"Now that's just what I like to hear." Doc beamed. "Good goin', son."

"What's he done that's so spectacular?"

Gabe jumped at Sarah's unexpected approach. "Uh…just telling Doc I'm prepared to do justice to some more of those desserts, soon as everyone else is ready for seconds."

"Oh, really? You might have a bit of a wait."

Mrs. G and Marissa followed her into the room.

Sarah claimed the easy chair beside Doc, leaving the recliner for Mrs. G. And the rest of the couch for Marissa. She hung back, sending Gabe a stern look from under her lowered lashes.

He knew full well she'd rather sit at the other end of the couch. But, to her credit, she settled on the cushion right beside him. So he circled his arm around her shoulders and held her against him.

"You're spoiled, Gabe Miller," Sarah said, "keeping Marissa all to yourself."

If only he could.

"And," she added, "we've decided it's high time you share the wealth. I get her first—she's going to give a cooking demonstration at the bookstore. Isn't that right, Marissa?"

"Yes, it is."

He glanced sideways at her, then pressed a quick kiss to her temple.

He'd hear about it later, he knew, recalling her claim that he got all the perks in this relationship—a crazy notion if ever he'd heard one.

Besides, it was Christmas, wasn't it?

"Sounds like a good plan."

"That's not all," Mrs. G put in. "We're going to have her run the dessert booth at the Founder's Day festival."

Not likely.

"Festival's in June. That's too long away to think about now, isn't it?" He stared down at Marissa.

"We'll see," she returned. "I haven't made any promises."

And everyone could interpret that whatever way they wanted.

She hadn't promised them she'd run the dessert booth. She hadn't promised him she'd stay. Or that she'd raise their child with him. She hadn't promised him anything.

What guarantee did he have that she'd stick around?

He couldn't let her go off and settle down in some unknown big city where she could change her mind about contacting him and he might never see her again.

Where he might never track down his child.

AT HOME in the ranch-house kitchen, Marissa smothered a yawn with one hand and set her bag of empty serving dishes on the counter near the sink.

"It's late, Gabe. I'm going to bed." She hung her coat on the peg beside his hat. "Just leave the dishes here. I'll get to them in the morning." Fighting another yawn, she left the kitchen and started down the hall.

"Hold on a bit," Gabe said. His boots hit the hardwood floor behind her, and he caught her in midstride, slipping his arm around her shoulders and swerving her course toward the living room. "Don't you want your present?"

Present? "We didn't say anything about exchanging gifts."

"What does that matter? Don't need permission to buy a little something for my wife, do I?"

"No…" Still, she couldn't help tensing beneath his guiding arm as he maneuvered her to the couch. As always, his nearness threatened her willpower and lowered her resolve.

Gabe crossed to the Christmas tree and pulled a green envelope from its branches. He must have slipped it in place while she was packing the food to take to Mrs. Gannett's. The envelope certainly hadn't been there when she sat daydreaming in front of the lit tree a few minutes before that.

He took a seat beside her on the couch and put the card on her lap.

"Thank you." She bit her lip, wishing she'd known to expect a gift, feeling awkward that she hadn't bought one for him.

She'd never had a card from Gabe before, not even on their wedding day. What had he chosen? A funny rhyme? A cute picture? A mushy verse, one that would tell her in another writer's words the feelings he could never bring himself to share?

Her hands shook as she turned the envelope over and lifted the flap. She held her breath and slid out the folded paper inside.

It wasn't a card.

Instead, she opened it to find a gift certificate from the local hardware store made out in her name. A nice gift, of course, but...

"They've got a huge decorating section," he told her. "All kinds of paint and wallpaper. Thought you might like to look there for the baby's room."

"Oh." He hadn't given up on the idea he had raised the night before. He *was* trying to make things work, in his own way. She smiled. "Thank you."

"That's not all. The manager's going to keep the store open late tomorrow night. Just for you."

"Oh, Gabe. How thoughtful." And it was.

The gift proved he was thinking about their child, a fact she truly cherished. The special arrangement proved her right—he did have two sides to him. The tough side, the armor, that he wouldn't let down in front of her. And the sensitive side, the sweetness, that he wouldn't let her see.

The confirmations made her crumple.

"Merry Christmas, Marissa," he said in the husky murmur that always threatened to undo her.

She reached out, wanting only to touch his cheek in a gesture of thanks. But he pressed his hand against hers, trapping her fingers against the warmth of his cheek, tantalizing her palm with the brush of his five-o'clock shadow.

Who was she kidding, thinking friendship with this man could ever be enough? It couldn't. Not when their relationship had started out red-hot, exploded to scorching, and continued to burn ember-bright inside her long after she had left him.

She couldn't stop herself from reaching up with her other hand to cup his face in hers. Couldn't stop him from wrapping his free arm around her waist and sliding her along the couch until they sat thigh-to-thigh against each other.

His lips brushed hers in an unspoken question. Her mouth joined his in a silent response. If he wouldn't give her the words she wanted, she would take what he offered and make of it what she could. She would read the language of his lips, his hands, his body, and satisfy herself with everything they so eloquently said.

She had to do something to justify her actions, to save her rapidly disintegrating self-esteem. Because, heaven help her, she was in danger of falling for Gabe Miller.

Again.

Something she would not allow to happen.

She couldn't give up everything she had fought so hard to accomplish. Wouldn't dismiss everything she so desperately needed to prove to herself. And absolutely refused to give in, yet again, to the sexual chemistry she had once mistaken for love.

Yet, right at that moment, she wanted to forget everything that had happened in the past, everything she wanted for the future, and simply focus on the present.

On the here and now, in Gabe's arms.

Chapter Twelve

Time was a-wasting this Saturday evening, when Gabe had places to go. People to see. A wife to court.

He'd waited all these hours already, this day after Christmas, to take Marissa to cash in her gift.

She didn't seem too eager, judging by the time she took to wipe down the counters, then fold the towel and center it on its hook. Stalling, it seemed—though he couldn't fathom why—and trying to avoid eye contact.

He frowned. "You about ready to head in to the hardware store?"

"Yes, I will be in—"

The telephone interrupted her. He crossed the room to answer it. The male voice at the other end sounded high-class and frosty-cold as it asked to speak to Marissa.

Gabe held out the receiver. "For you."

Curiosity kept him from leaving. Heck, he owned the place. If she didn't want him to overhear, she knew the location of every phone in the house. He took the nearest chair and tuned in to the conversation. It didn't take long to find out the first thing he wanted to know—who was this stranger calling his wife?

"F-Father?" Her voice rose.

Shock or maybe fear, judging by the way her eyes darted around the room, as if afraid the man might appear there.

"How did—? I mean, Merry Christmas. I— No, I didn't— I was planning to but—"

He could've sighed in frustration. It sure wouldn't satisfy much curiosity, if she kept this up. Then, even worse, she gave up on the chopped-off attempts at speech and switched to a wide-eyed stare. At nothing.

After a long silence, she blurted, "How did you find—?" Her face went as white as the pastry dough she'd made Christmas morning. That brought him to his feet.

He moved to stand beside her, hovering near her elbow, not sure she even knew he was there.

"And that's all I am to you, Father?" she burst out. "Just one of your employees?" Another silence, this one seeming to stretch on and on. Then she gasped, her eyes brightened, and her fingers on the receiver turned as colorless as her face. "No! That's not true! I'm not—" Her voice broke.

So did Gabe's heart. Where did this guy get off, upsetting her like this? Before he could think things through, he snatched the phone from her unresisting hand.

"What's going on here?" he barked into the receiver.

"*I* am Marissa's father." The voice had dropped a few notches to a deep-freeze. "And *this* is a private conversation."

"Yeah? Well, *I* am Marissa's husband. And *this* is the sound of me hanging up on you." He slammed the receiver into the cradle. The thought hit him, too late, that Marissa might not have appreciated the interference. He didn't much care. He'd have hung up on the bigheaded SOB regardless.

He took his seat and shot a glance her way.

She stared back, her face still ghostly pale, her eyes wide and watery, one stray teardrop caught on her lower lashes. As he watched, her mouth twisted in silent fury and he waited for the tongue-lashing he knew would follow.

But instead she gave way to a cross between a hiccup and a giggle.

He narrowed his eyes. "Something funny?"

"You." She giggled some more. "What you did. I can't believe you hung up on him."

"If he talked to you the same way he talked to me, he deserved it. And he must have, seeing how you reacted."

As if he'd doused her with cold water—or she'd just recalled that unfeeling voice on the phone—she sobered. "That was my father."

"So I gathered."

"And that's pretty much how he speaks to anyone who displeases him."

"Knowing you're married and expecting 'displeases him'?" He took his anger out on the salt and pepper shakers in front of him, shoving them to one side of the table.

"That's not it. He still doesn't know about the baby."

"Someone must've told him."

She shook her head. "No one knows. Being the owner's daughter doesn't earn you too many friends. No one in Father's empire knows I'm pregnant." She refused to meet his eyes. "I didn't think he'd even know yet that I quit my job because I'd gotten married. That's all he would say when I asked how he knew," she added bitterly, her voice shaking. "'You *know* I keep up-to-date information on *anyone* in my employ.'"

She sank into a chair at the other end of the table, her expression blank. Closed to him. "He'll never forgive me."

He snorted. "For what? Quitting? Getting married? Not inviting him to the wedding?"

"For not conforming to what he wants me to be." She sighed. "He didn't have any control over me when I was growing up, no say in how I was raised. And so, no interest in me." Her voice grew more bitter, her eyes lost focus, as if she'd left the ranch-house kitchen and gone back in time. "I had to beg him to let me live with him when I turned sixteen. He didn't want me at all."

"I won't argue the point with you, Marissa." He kept his voice low, wanting to bring her back from the hurtful memories. "Bad things happen in life, like having a parent desert you. If you're lucky, you hold even tighter to the people still there. You were lucky. You had your mother."

Her head shot up. He'd said exactly the wrong thing.

"Sorry, Gabe, you don't know what you're talking about."

He did know, in a way. But this time he kept his mouth shut.

"You remember I told you my mother and I never had a Christmas tree? Because we moved around too much?"

He nodded.

"We moved so often because my mother couldn't settle down for very long. As in, stay with one man for more than a few months." Shaking her head, she added, "Mother changed men more often than I changed my mind about what I wanted to do when I grew up. And trust me, I didn't always know I wanted to be a chef. That came gradually, after years of doing the cooking for the two of us and the latest lover." She toyed with the salt shaker he had pushed aside, passing it from hand to hand.

"Oh, she loved each and every one of them. For as long as the feeling lasted." She laughed without humor. "She couldn't have married any of them, anyway. Oh, no. Give up the monthly alimony check that managed to reach her no matter how often we moved? Because, of course, Father kept tabs. I'm sure he was as good then as he is now at gathering background information."

She tilted the salt shaker, dribbling white crystals almost grain by grain onto the tabletop. Just as she was dropping one heartbreaking fact after another.

He thought about stopping the conversation. But maybe talking about her past helped push away thoughts of the present—and that telephone call.

"And of course—" her hand shook, sending a shower

of salt onto the table "—she couldn't have let me live with Father. No, that would mean giving up the monthly child-support check."

"I don't—"

"Please don't tell me you think that couldn't be true. I know what she thought. I know what she did. I know what she let happen, for the sake of that extra check."

Under the edge of the table, he fisted his hands against his thighs, sure he knew what was coming and not certain at all he could block his reaction.

"I'm surprised she wasn't jealous that some of her boyfriends paid so much attention to me. Or maybe she was. Maybe that's why, when it happened once too often and I managed to get Father to agree to let me live with him, she didn't offer a protest."

"Sweetheart, I'm sorry." Sorry wasn't good enough, but what more could he say?

She cupped a hand at the table's edge and swept the loose salt into her palm, then closed her fingers in a white-knuckled fist. "It seems Father felt I needed to hear that I'm just like my mother."

"That's crazy talk, Marissa. Why'd he say that? You left behind a string of men?"

"Of course not."

"Then what?"

After a long pause, she shook her head. "I think it's because I no longer work for him. That takes away his control."

"Sounds to me like you're better off without him."

"Am I?"

"Sure. And maybe you've got no other family, no other place to go. But you've got a place here."

He'd blurted out the statement without giving it a moment's thought. Which didn't matter, because he meant it. He felt for her, having such a jerk as a parent.

Much as he'd missed his mama and had suffered from not having her around, Marissa had run up against a whole other situation. She would have been better off never getting involved with her daddy to begin with. Then again, she'd have been stuck with another worthless parent.

All the more reason for their own child to grow up in a good environment. On the ranch. With two parents.

Couldn't Marissa see that?

As HE ENTERED Dillon, instead of heading for the hardware store, Gabe turned the pickup toward the diner. He needed some time. Some breathing room. Some of Delia's high-test.

Marissa had taken that stupid phone call to heart. And she'd been distant to him all the way to town. He'd tried to distract her, cheer her up, make things right.

But she'd been so hurt by her own daddy, she hadn't paid him any notice.

He suspected the man had money, enough to help her rustle his own ranch out from under him. But somehow, after listening to her talk, he doubted that was her aim. She had too much pride to ask her father for anything.

Inside the crowded diner, everybody greeted him and Marissa like an old married couple. Which they wouldn't get to be, if he didn't make up his mind and do something about it.

He nodded at Delia and grabbed gratefully at the mug she'd filled when they'd come in the door.

"Hey," he said to Marissa, "Doc and Mrs. G are down back in Doc's usual corner. Let's go join them."

"Fine." She led the way.

"Well, look who's here," Doc said.

Mrs. G moved over on her bench seat and slid her dinner plate along with her.

Marissa took the empty space.

Gabe took a wooden chair from the next table and set it at the end of the booth, close enough to Marissa to reach out and take her hand. She didn't pull away. She wouldn't, in front of company. But she was still quieter than usual.

He didn't like it. He had to do something to make her forget the phone call. He squeezed her hand. "We're glad we ran into you tonight, aren't we, honey?"

"Yes." She gave a small smile, probably for the benefit of Doc and Mrs. G.

"Marissa and I've got some good news." Her hand tensed in his. "I'll come right out with it—we're having a baby."

Mrs. G gasped. "How wonderful! My dear, when can we expect the new arrival?"

"The beginning of June," Marissa answered, her voice soft.

Her cheeks had turned pink, but her smile warmed. She turned to answer a slew of questions from his old schoolteacher.

Across the table, Doc winked at him.

Gabe sat back in his chair and took a big swig of coffee.

He listened to Marissa rattle on about the baby. She sounded happy. Anyone could tell that. Her happiness, and Doc's assurances about the pregnancy, made him finally certain.

She hadn't lied about being pregnant.

It stood to reason she wouldn't lie about him being the father, either. Truth to tell, he'd believed that all along, though he'd only let himself admit it a short while ago. He'd listened too long to his fear, when he should've been heeding Marissa.

We're having a baby.

The same words she had said to him the morning she'd come back. The same reason, more than ever now, she needed to stay.

But would she?

He thought back to all she'd said about her life, the way she had lived in her early years, how she had gone from town to town as her mother moved from man to man. Would Marissa repeat the pattern? Hadn't she, already, by leaving?

Suddenly, Delia's high-test tasted bitter.

DOC WATCHED as Gabe and Marissa left the diner. A split second later, Lily Gannett signaled across the room.

Delia started toward them, having the presence of mind to remember the coffeepot. She plopped into the chair Gabe had left at the end of the booth. Years of practice had her refilling Doc's coffee without spilling a drop, even though she'd locked eyes with Lily. Doc reached gratefully for the mug.

"Delia," Lily said in a hushed voice. "You'll never guess. Gabe and Marissa are on their way to the hardware store to pick out wallpaper—for their baby's room!"

"She's pregnant?"

"She is. And Gabe's pleased as punch about it."

"Then maybe we're wrong?" Delia's brow wrinkled. "Sounds like everything's fine and dandy, after all."

He sipped coffee, considering.

Gabe seemed fit to bust at sharing the news, but he knew the boy well enough to detect something still forced about the enthusiasm. Marissa, he didn't know well at all, but that day she'd come in to his office, he'd seen both happiness and excitement. He'd seen a bit of that tonight, too. But, every once in a while, she'd looked distracted…and upset, to boot.

Lily seemed to have read his mind. "No, Delia. Something's not right. They're sleeping in separate rooms."

Doc gaped at her. "How in tarnation did you find that out?"

She had the grace to blush. "I didn't ask, if that's what you're thinking."

"So, how?" Delia demanded.

"When we went out to the ranch earlier this week, you know, for the candy-making lesson, I…um…needed to powder my nose. And when I went down the hallway, I passed the guest room. You know yourself, Doc," she added pointedly, "you need to pass Gabe's guest room to get to the washroom."

"All right," he agreed. "On with the story."

"The door was open, and I happened to look in, and I saw definite signs that a woman was staying in the room."

"And Marissa's the only woman on that ranch," Delia put in.

He shrugged. "Maybe she uses it for sewing, or crafts—"

"A *bed*room." The schoolteacher voice brooked no argument.

"Well, dang." Deep in thought, Delia automatically topped off Doc's coffee mug and set the pot down again. "Then that means there's still something wrong."

"Yes. And now that we know they're having a child, it's more important than ever to make sure Marissa stays on the ranch."

"Yeah," Delia said. "It'd sure help, though, if they'd share the same bed."

Even Doc had to agree with both of those statements.

Lily sighed. "I don't see how we could accomplish that."

She looked frustrated, Delia, fretful.

And Marissa, he reminded himself, had looked upset and distracted. Couldn't be about the baby on the way, so it had to have something to do with Gabe.

They'd kept a distance during the party at his house—at least, till Delia had invented the mistletoe. And they'd mostly sidestepped each other at Lily's on Christmas.

No way for newlyweds to behave. The more time they spent with each other, the better their chances of getting comfortable, and then of working things out.

Nothing else would do with a baby on the way.

He swallowed his last mouthful of coffee, set down his mug, and said, "All right. I reckon I can do something that'll get them together…."

As GABE HELD the door for her on their way out of the diner, Marissa could barely contain her anger. She couldn't pull away; at this hour on a Saturday evening, they had too many interested pairs of eyes turned in their direction. But she'd be darned if she'd smile up adoringly at him.

The second they were well clear of the diner, she exploded. "Why did you tell Doc and Mrs. Gannett about the baby when I had asked that we not say anything?"

Gabe wrapped an arm around her shoulders and laughed. "Honey, we're visiting the hardware store to pick out baby wallpaper. You think the manager's not going to put two and two together? You think he's not going to talk?"

"Everybody in this town talks," she muttered. "Except you."

Gabe didn't answer. She wasn't surprised.

Anger at him mixed with her own guilt.

Fleetingly, she thought of Sarah Jones. But she hadn't *told* her anything. Sarah had guessed.

She felt guilty, too, about how much she had enjoyed discussing babies and bottles and layettes with Mrs. Gannett. How natural it had felt, and how special.

This life growing inside her *was* special.

It was her own life that had gotten so messed up. And she blamed herself. If she hadn't jumped into marriage without getting to know Gabe first, things would be so different right now.

Chapter Thirteen

At the hardware store, Gabe swept the front door open for Marissa.

Inside, the manager greeted them with a wide, friendly smile, as if the grapevine had already spread the good news.

If it had, he said nothing about it. Instead, he escorted her to a row of stools in front of a long wooden counter. Wallpaper sample books had already been arranged on the countertop.

She took a seat and, with trembling fingers, opened the cover of the nearest sampler.

"Guess I'll leave you to it," Gabe said. He stood beside her, one booted foot resting on a rung of the stool. "I've got to get a few things down in back of the store."

She looked up at him in surprise, then almost wished she hadn't. Before dinner, he had showered and changed into a crisp white shirt and worn jeans that showed off his toned body. He looked more appetizing than ever, no matter how much he frustrated her.

"You aren't planning to look at wallpaper with me?" Readying the room for the baby had been his idea.

"Nah. I've got no talent for that kind of thing."

She frowned. "Or do you mean no interest?"

He laughed and leaned forward to nuzzle her cheek. "I've got plenty of interest whenever you're concerned, honey."

She could have screamed. He was teasing her for the sake of the all-too-curious manager standing nearby. She gripped the wallpaper sampler and willed herself not to react. A moot point, as she didn't know how to respond, anyway. Fresh emotions bombarded her in a struggle between the desire to escape from him and…

And just plain desire.

"Got plenty of things I want to do with you, too," he continued, his breath tickling her ear, this time his words low enough for her alone to hear. "But we'd best not go into that right now." He chuckled, then swaggered away.

She smoothed the crumpled page she'd been holding. Her fingers were trembling again, this time from despair.

Since their kiss the night before, she'd felt shaky inside, as if she'd swallowed a liter of seltzer in one long gulp and now couldn't catch her breath.

She'd spent all day in dreams, each more dangerous than the last. Wishful thinking. Impossible imaginings. Vain hopes that things would work out between them, not just for the baby's sake, but for her own.

Daydreams weren't real. Neither was her marriage, not based as it was—always had been—on sexual attraction.

She couldn't blame Gabe entirely. They had both jumped willingly into the relationship. Only, she had wanted love, sharing, commitment; the cowboy she'd married wanted a continuous roll in the hay.

She had to remember that.

And the phone call from Father, with its face-slapping dose of reality, wouldn't let her forget.

"Just what did you know about this man, Marissa, before you fell into his bed?"

Nothing, Father. But shame had stilled her tongue.

"There's a word for girls like you."

Shock kept her silent.

"You're no better than your mother, Marissa."

She'd gasped. *"No! That's not true! I'm not—"* She had broken off mid-sentence, unable to defend herself and deny the truth. She *was* just like her mother.

And for that, she and Gabe and their baby would suffer.

Tears prickled behind her eyes. The wallpaper pattern blurred.

Already, the baby suffered.

At the diner earlier, Gabe had acted proud and happy, and now he couldn't even bother to help with decorating ideas for their child's room.

Because at the diner, he'd had an audience in the form of Mrs. Gannett and Doc.

He was following the terms of their agreement to the letter: he needed to perform only in front of other people. Terms she had agreed to, she admitted, fighting to hold back a sob.

"Marissa?"

The sound of his voice made her jump. By his tone, it was obvious he'd spoken to her more than once.

"Got something for you, sweetheart." On the counter in front of her, he placed a large box gift-wrapped in red satiny paper and decorated with gold ribbon and a gold lace bow. "Ordered it for Christmas. It didn't get here till today."

Is that why he'd hurried off to the back of the store?

She glanced over his shoulder but didn't see the manager anywhere within listening distance.

"Go on, open it," Gabe urged, studying her.

Looking down, she concentrated on tearing open the Christmas wrap, using it as camouflage to hide her shaking hands.

A final sweep of the paper, and her present from Gabe stood revealed: a set of professional—and very expensive—French cookware.

For a moment, she sat speechless. Again, this wasn't the romantic, heartfelt gift she had hoped for. Still, it proved Gabe was thinking about her and her interests, just as the gift certificate showed he'd thought about their child.

She gave him a big smile. "Thank you."

"Knew *this* would do the trick," he murmured.

The words, along with his smug grin, tipped her off. His chest, puffed with pride, underscored the message. Her husband was courting her. Not because he wanted to, but because they had made a deal.

This wasn't a gift given from a man who loved his

wife and wanted to please her, from a man who gave from the heart.

It was an installment payment on their agreement.

She gasped in shock at the thought, then hurriedly smiled again to make it seem an exclamation of pleasure.

Gabe beamed, unaware of her ragged emotions and of the disturbing idea that had just shot through her.

If his courtship was real—and successful—what would he want from her in return? Would he feel entitled to take their pretend marriage to the next step...and expect her to share his bed?

GABE DUG INTO Marissa's special Sunday-morning breakfast of French toast and sausages. As he ate, he contemplated the day ahead, and how he'd spend it cozying up to his wife. If he could get close enough to her.

Last night, she'd seemed pleased enough when he'd given her the one-day-late Christmas gift. Then she'd turned all quiet on him again.

And this morning, every time he went near her, she managed to have an urgent need for something in the refrigerator or a cabinet on the other side of the room.

Danged if he'd ever understand women.

He downed the last of his French toast and pushed his plate aside. Then he rose and headed over to Marissa. When he put his hands on her shoulders, she tensed.

"Boys."

He said the word once, loud enough that they all quieted down. "We got some news for y'all this morning."

Marissa pulled away from his hands and stood up. For one awful moment, he expected her to stomp out of the room. To give his friends yet another reason to pity him.

Instead, she moved to his side and smiled up at him.

Sweet and natural and sexy as all get-out.

He wrapped his arm around her, held her close, and turned to grin at his cowhands. "Come summertime, we're gonna have another mouth to feed around here."

"Yee-hah!" yelled Eddie.

The other men slapped high fives.

"Hey, Warren?" The older man looked stunned and a bit red around the eyes. Gabe blinked a couple times and cleared his throat before continuing. "You with us?"

"Sure am, boss." He pushed himself up from the table and shook Gabe's hand. His face spread in a grin wider than Gabe had ever seen on him before. "I'm buying the first pair of boots for that young'un, now, you hear me?"

Gabe and Marissa laughed.

"Sure thing, old man."

Warren's wrinkled face turned bright red. "And I get first congrats with the missus, too."

To Gabe's astonishment, he leaned over and kissed Marissa's cheek. That cleared the way for the rest of the hands, who lined up for their own turns. By the time they were done, she was as red-faced as Warren.

"Anything we can do you for you, Marissa, you just holler," Jared told her.

"Funny you should mention that," she answered. "Actually, I could use some help in the house today."

"No problem."

Gabe frowned. He'd intended to keep busy with her in the house today, but his plans sure didn't include the boys. "Help doing what?"

"There are a lot of boxes and pieces of furniture in Gabe's old bedroom that need to be moved up to the attic."

"Hey," he said, "I can handle that."

"Some of the pieces are too big for one person, but I don't think I—"

"Don't worry, missus," Warren broke in, "we'll be happy to pitch in, won't we, boys?"

Gabe gave serious thought to putting his old friend out to pasture.

"Sure, we'll help," Eddie added, "especially if you're still planning to make that Boston cream pie you mentioned yesterday."

"Are you sure it will be worth a day of hard labor?" Marissa laughed and put her hands on her hips. The movement pulled her sweater tight, outlining her breasts. Hitting Gabe where it hurt. And making him think of things they'd once done up in his bedroom in the main house. Things he wanted to do now.

Not likely he'd get a chance, though, judging by how fast the boys had jumped up to help clear the table so they could head on over with them.

Damn. The frustrations of playacting this marriage just might kill him.

MARISSA SHIFTED position on the floor of Gabe's old bedroom and settled back against the oak dresser. Nowadays, she tired so easily, and her back twinged from time to time.

She pulled the cardboard carton beside her a little closer.

They had all worked hard yesterday, emptying the room.

She hadn't found any wallpaper that appealed to her, so she had decided to paint instead. Warren had gone into town with her today to pick up the supplies they needed.

She planned to get started setting up the room right away. With any luck, she could shift Gabe's focus away from her—away from sex—and make him see what was most important.

Their child.

She looked down at the box of mementos she had found pushed far back on the upper shelf of the closet. Obviously, they were keepsakes saved from Gabe's childhood.

Thoughts of their own child so overwhelmed her, her eyes misted.

In his phone call, Father had shamed her with his accusation that she had followed in her mother's footsteps. And she'd secretly acknowledged that truth. Yet, deep in her heart, she knew she deserved so much more. The telephone call from Father had made her finally understand.

She wanted to stay on the ranch.

All along, she'd known in her heart that her baby

deserved a better life than she'd had herself. Her baby deserved a happy home. A loving mother and father. A family.

She and Gabe couldn't build that family if they couldn't develop a friendship first. And what were the chances of that, with the fake relationship they had created?

She ran her hand along the box of mementos.

She would fight for her child, would find something positive in this mess she had made of her life. And by putting words to her determination, she found the tiniest glimmer of hope.

Maybe, just maybe, Gabe's willingness to help her with the baby's room, along with his thoughtful Christmas gifts, meant he had begun to care for her a little.

She prayed for that to be true. For the contents of this box to help him open up to her. And to bring them, finally and forever, together.

GABE QUIT EARLY, determined to get time alone with his wife. Yesterday, he couldn't have beaten the boys off with a stick, if he'd wanted to.

He'd spent most of today out with them, then gotten back to the barn in late afternoon, only to learn from Warren about Marissa's change in plans. And that she'd asked the older man to accompany her to town.

Seems she'd do anything to avoid being with *him*.

All the irritation of the day before came back. She'd managed to keep her distance from him most of the time, through dinner and supper and the Boston cream pie for dessert. And in the evening, she'd disappeared before he could turn around.

No way would he let that happen today.

He took a quick shower in the bunkhouse, then headed on over to the main house and up the stairs to the second floor.

In the doorway of his old room, now filled with paint buckets and rollers, he stumbled to a halt and looked across at his wife.

Seeing her, kneeling in front of a low oak dresser she was covering with a plastic cloth, kind of put a damper on any heat he'd generated the day before. Probably because the dresser had once overflowed with T-shirts and boys' briefs, plastic horses and Tonka trucks.

Soon it would be filled with diapers and tiny booties and what all a baby would need. The thought brought a lump to his throat, and he coughed to clear it.

Marissa jumped. "Oh, Gabe." She smiled. "I didn't see you there."

"Like I hardly saw you yesterday."

"What are you talking about?" One hand against her back, she rose to her feet. "We were together almost all day."

"Yeah, just one big happy family."

She winced. "Warren and the boys were a lot of help. We couldn't have made nearly as much progress with just the two of us. And it was your idea to set up this room for the baby. If you've changed your mind…"

More likely, she wanted to change hers. Any excuse

would do, so long as it didn't tie her to the ranch. He crossed the room in two strides and stood in front of her. "I haven't. What about you?"

"N-no."

"I'm here to help. Warren said you're not papering now."

She nodded. "I decided to paint. But I'm not going to start until tomorrow."

"You're not going to start at all."

"So you have changed your mind."

He shook his head. "Nope."

"If you think I don't have any experience, you're right." She raised her chin. "But I'll learn as I go along."

"Not this time. Paint fumes aren't good for pregnant women. Warren and I'll do the painting."

"Oh." Her jaw lowered a few notches. She smiled again, and he had to fight to keep from reaching out to her. "In that case, thank you. I'll just finish covering this bureau, then go over to the bunkhouse to start supper."

"I'll help."

Together they wrapped the piece of furniture with the plastic, tucking it in on all sides.

She looked around. "Now that we moved the overflow out of here, I can see what a nice room this is."

One boot propped on a cardboard box, he leaned back against the wall. "Yeah, I always liked this place. Window's a little low because of the sloped ceiling—made it easy to climb out and down the tree outside."

"Climb out?" She looked up, her eyes wide. "Didn't your father have a fit when he found out what you'd done?"

"Granddaddy wanted to, sure enough." He shrugged. "But Daddy told him it helped a boy grow a sense of independence."

"And did it?"

"Sure. Only he wasn't happy to hear Daddy used to sneak out that way all the time." He laughed, but Marissa frowned.

She looked at the windowsill, just inches above the floor. "It doesn't seem safe enough to put a baby—"

"Hold on," he interrupted. Was she looking for excuses again? "It's plenty safe. And if you're worried, we can put one of those gates on the window."

"I guess you're right."

"Sure I am." For emphasis, he shoved the cardboard box away from him and stood tall.

She looked down at the box. "Oh, that reminds me." She came over to kneel beside him. "I found this carton in the closet. I didn't know if you wanted to put it up in the attic or keep it down here."

"Can't think there's much of anything in there I'd want."

"I think you'll be surprised." Her smile lit her face.

Damn, but she was beautiful. The hell with acting— he wanted some *action*. He wanted her. In his arms and in his bed.

She reached for the box, and he hunkered down on his boot heels. It brought him closer to her.

She opened the lid, and he wished he'd stayed farther away.

His hands turned clammy. His stomach dropped to his boots.

Funny, how memory could fool you.

He'd have bet money he'd never seen that box before. But as soon as he laid eyes on the contents, he knew he'd not only seen that carton, he'd hoarded every last blasted item in it.

Taken one out after dark, when Daddy and Granddaddy wouldn't see. Cried with it under the covers, where Daddy and Granddaddy wouldn't hear. Put it away every morning, so Daddy and Granddaddy wouldn't know.

One at a time. All he could handle.

One every night of his little-boy life.

Yeah, memory could fool you.

People could, too.

If you let them.

Chapter Fourteen

Holding her breath, Marissa looked into the open box. She had so much at stake here, had mixed so many dreams amid this little collection of loving mementos.

With a trembling smile, she looked at Gabe. He crouched beside her, unmoving, staring down at the carton, an indescribable look in his eyes. She was touched by his obvious emotion at seeing the family keepsakes.

She prayed that, one day soon, he would feel that same power of emotion for their own child. And for her.

Smiling, she reached for the ceramic frame that sat on top of the pile. The picture inside the frame showed a woman cradling a newborn.

"Your mother, Gabe? She's beautiful. You've got her eyes."

His were now dark and smoldering, and his reaction at seeing the picture touched her even more. He'd had the family she'd always wanted, the closeness with parents she'd always craved. The relationship she so desperately wanted for her baby.

She had to blink hard and look away from him, down at the frame again. Still conscious of him beside her, she ran her thumb along the ceramic edge and imagined a picture of her cradling his child.

"Your mom saved so many keepsakes for you. I'll bet it's been a while since you've seen them. Look." She reached for the next few items in the box and placed them on the floor around their feet.

A pair of knitted blue booties and a matching cap. A finger-painted drawing of a purple-spotted horse. A miniature pair of cowboy boots. And a little log cabin made of Popsicle sticks.

"I'll bet she knitted the cap and booties for you, didn't she? And how sweet to save them all for—"

"No." He shot to his feet.

She looked up at him. "What's the—"

"She didn't save them. Daddy and Granddaddy must have. I told them to throw 'em all out."

"Gabe." She rose to stand beside him, reached out to touch his arm. Tension radiated from his body, from the drawn lines around his eyes. For once, she didn't react to the feel of him with a physical response, but with a purely emotional one, a heart-wrenching throb of sympathy.

"I'm sorry. I didn't know it would affect you this way to see these things again." She tightened her grip. "It must have been hard, losing your mother. But you shouldn't pack all these memories away. You're so lucky to have these mementos—"

He laughed, a guttural gust of sound without a trace of humor. "Give it up, Marissa. You're the one with the happy-family fantasy. Don't try transferring it onto me. I didn't 'lose' my mother. She lost me. Me and Daddy and Granddaddy."

"I don't understand—"

"I was six years old—not even Kevin's age—when she walked out on us." He dropped his arms to his sides, pulling her hand free of his wrist. "She took off. Left. Vamoosed. You get the idea. Here one day, gone the next. And I never saw her again."

Coldness swept through her. She knew what his words implied—a connection between his mother's desertion and her own leaving. What could she ever do that would make things better between them? What could she ever say that would take away his pain?

Tears filled her eyes. Through the sudden blur, she saw him clench his fists. Saw the cords in his neck tighten, a vein in his temple pulse, raw fury turn his eyes black.

"Funny, women don't seem to stick around this place."

"I'm still here," she whispered, her voice cracking.

"Yeah." His eyes glinted, sharp as the hard steel blade of a boning knife. "For how long?"

She tried to speak, but words clogged in her throat. She couldn't respond, when she didn't know the answer.

Even now, no matter how much her heart hurt for him, no matter how much she wanted to stay, she couldn't make promises she might not keep.

He moved away, his foot lashing against the box, skidding it across the floor. He took another step. She heard something crunch beneath his boot.

Looking straight ahead, he strode across the room, his heels shaking the walls. Or maybe her ragged breaths and wobbly legs and heaving stomach made things seem to move around her.

Slowly, she sank to her knees.

On the floor beside her lay a little log cabin made of Popsicle sticks now splintered beyond repair.

Swallowing a sob, she bowed her head, closed her eyes and covered her face with her hands.

SHE HADN'T yet recovered from his emotional revelation the day before. It had made Marissa wary of being close to him again, uncertain about how she should act, and completely unable to figure out what he was feeling or thinking—something he certainly wouldn't tell her now. He wasn't ready for that. He might never be.

The thought filled her with sorrow.

Still, he had shared something with her, painful though it might be. And she'd gained some insight into what made Gabe the man he was.

She spent the morning in the kitchen, only once venturing upstairs, where Gabe and Warren had started work in the baby's room.

She stood just outside the doorway.

"You've almost finished the first coat," she noted, pleased by their progress. She waved at a pale green wall. "How do you like it so far?"

"Nice and cheerful," Warren said. "But I'm going to need those brushes from the barn to take care of that sloped corner."

Before she could react, he had slipped past her, leaving her alone with Gabe, who stood wielding a long-handled roller, applying a coat of color to a wall with slow, even strokes. He wore a pair of jeans worn through in places and an old faded T-shirt to do the painting, and beneath the T-shirt's sleeves, his biceps flexed with his movements.

For a breathless second, she stood transfixed, drinking in the sight of him. Then she blinked and pulled her gaze away.

He hadn't answered her question. Hadn't even turned around to face her.

"What do you think about the color, Gabe?" she persisted.

"Warren called it."

She held back a sigh. "I've got a border, too."

"Sounds good." He knelt to set his roller down on a paint tray. More bunching and flexing, this time the play of strong muscles in his thighs and calves. Her mouth grew dry.

He rose again, and now, he did turn to face her. And more. He stepped carefully across the paint-spattered drop cloth on the floor.

She wouldn't turn and flee, no matter how much she wanted to avoid being close to him. But she couldn't help backing up a step.

He kept coming.

"Uh…we'll need a second coat," she blurted. "But I'm glad now that I chose the light color. It will change the atmosphere of this room completely."

And maybe chase away some of Gabe's bad memories.

At the moment she wished she could chase him away, too.

Still, he moved closer, and her heart started to pound.

"You ought not to be in here."

"You're right. The paint." She retreated into the middle of the hall. He stopped in the doorway. "You should be done by early this afternoon," she continued. "I want to look for a crib."

"Right away?"

"You said yourself, I'll soon be halfway through the pregnancy." And the sooner Gabe started thinking of her as a wife *and* mother of his child, the better. For all three of them.

"Special order?"

She shook her head. "No, I thought I'd just take a look in the nearest department store."

"About thirty miles away."

"My car can handle the trip." She chose her next words carefully. "Of course, your truck would work better if I buy something that can be brought home immediately. If you and Warren finish early enough this afternoon, maybe you could go along with me."

She held her breath, waiting. Hoping.

Finally, he answered. "Yeah, I can do that."

For a moment, his features softened with feelings she wasn't sure she could put into words. Then the moment was gone, and he was stepping back into the room and out of her view.

She started down the stairs. Halfway along, a thought hit her, stealing her breath. She halted and grasped the railing.

She knew now what Gabe's face had shown. Emotions she had never seen in him before.

Yearning. Wanting. And need.

Not hot and steamy. Not sexual at all. Those, she would have recognized right away.

Instead, she had seen concern in his expression. In his actions, too, when he had cautioned her about leaving the freshly painted room.

Were his feelings all for the baby? Or did he care about her, too?

Was it possible that, deep in his heart, where he felt all the things he couldn't say, he wanted *her* to stay?

THEY WERE OUT of town and back with a crib in less time than Marissa had thought possible.

Warren had heard them pull up and was already there, opening the tailgate.

"It's a beautiful crib," she told him. "A sweet little oak four-poster that perfectly matches Gabe's bureau. And it converts to a twin bed, too. You're going to love it."

"Yeah?"

She laughed. "Well, *I* like it."

"Let's get this set up," Gabe said.

"Right now?"

"Good a time as any."

Gabe had been quiet but pleasant during the whole trip.

Though she had asked his opinion about her selection, he left the decision up to her. She tried not to let
that bother her. Tried instead to hold on to the hopes he
had unknowingly given her. By his interest in setting up
the crib so soon. And, even more, by the emotions he
had let slip through his guard.

"All right." She went ahead of the men to open the
kitchen door, then stayed downstairs to start preparing supper.

A while later, she heard Gabe calling her. "Come and
take a quick look."

As she peered into the baby's room, tears came to her
eyes. "Oh," she said softly, "you even put on the sheet
and bumpers."

"Yeah. Too soon to leave them up for good, but we
thought we'd surprise you."

And she was surprised, yet again, by this evidence
of his tender side. Was it wrong to want to see that more
often? "It's beautiful," she told them. "Just perfect."

"Looks good," Warren agreed. "And done just in
time to get washed up for supper, too."

"Yeah," Gabe said forcefully.

Marissa laughed.

Warren departed, leaving her alone again with Gabe.

She waved a hand, indicating the room, and
murmured, "So what do you think?"

He looked around. "Made a big difference."

If only it could make a lasting difference in him, the
way it already had in her. She could see a baby nestled in
that crib. Could feel what it would be like to be a family.

When Gabe picked up the cans of leftover paint he planned to take out to the barn, she led the way down the stairs. Halfway along the hall, she heard the telephone ring.

"I got it," Warren yelled.

In the kitchen, they found him in enthusiastic conversation.

"Looks right nice, too. You'd never know it was Gabe's old room. Yeah, right here. Hang on a minute, Doc." He held out the receiver to Gabe, waved to Marissa and left the kitchen.

She turned to the refrigerator. They needed extra milk at the bunkhouse, and another tomato or two.

Idly, she listened to Gabe's conversation, which consisted mostly of, "Yeah, Doc." "Sure...sure."

Never very talkative, he was practically speechless on a telephone. Yet he didn't need many words when he wanted to get a message across. She almost smiled, thinking of him hanging up on Father. She would pay for that one day, of course, but for now she found it very satisfying.

"No problem, Doc. We'll be home this evening, for sure." Gabe replaced the receiver and looked over at her.

"Is Doc planning to drop by tonight?" she asked.

"Yeah."

Gabe's sudden smile looked...funny. Hard to describe. Excited? Elated? Maybe a little smug?

She put her hands on her hips. Immediately, his attention swung to that part of her anatomy, then began to travel slowly up her body, sending a rush of warmth through her. Knowing her cheeks were flushed, she turned away.

"So what's going on?"

"Doc's bringing company."

"To supper? How nice." She began thinking about what she might add to tonight's menu.

"No, not to supper. To stay."

She whirled to face him. "Stay? Where? Not here?"

"Oh, yeah. Seems he's got an overflow of people coming to town for New Year's and needs a place to put them up."

"You didn't tell him he could bring them here?" Gabe's smug smile widened, and she knew he had done just that. "You can't. We have no place to put them. Unless…" Her mind worked feverishly, calculating something much more critical than what to serve for supper. "If they're all male, they can sleep in the bunkhouse."

Gabe stood shaking his head. "Nope. Married couple, Doc said."

"Okay, then, I'll sleep in the baby's room."

In an instant, he stood before her. She refused to back off, forced herself to meet his gaze.

"Can't, Marissa. Fresh paint, remember? Besides, no extra beds, no extra mattresses. And—" he glared at her "—no way someone's going to find out we're in separate rooms."

"They won't." She couldn't give in to this arrangement, knowing it might take her somewhere she wasn't ready to go. Not yet. Please, not yet. Not until she had proved herself.

"Our agreement, remember?"

She groaned. How could she forget?

"One small detail," he persisted. "We agreed about not sharing a bed, but the deal didn't say one damned word about sleeping in the same room. I kept my end of the bargain."

And, heaven help her, she needed to keep hers.

She caved in. What else could she do? "All right. I'll move into your room. We'll take turns sleeping on the floor."

"Hell, no," he snapped. "Not me, not you. Circumstances change and we've got to adapt, that's all."

"Gabe—"

"Forget it. My house, I sleep in my bed. And I won't have a pregnant woman sleeping on the floor."

In an instant, all the happiness of her day trickled away. All the worries came flooding back.

How could they form a friendship first, when they would be sleeping together in one bedroom?

Chapter Fifteen

Frowning, Gabe sipped his fresh cup of coffee.

They'd had Doc's guests in the main house for a couple nights now. By rights, that *should've* worked in his favor. He'd been happy to help out Doc, to let the man's friends take over Marissa's bedroom. Their arrival had put her in his room, in his bed—where he wanted her.

Yet she had turned all his plans against him.

By day, she'd busied herself with cooking and baking for the late New Year's Eve supper she'd just set out for his men. By night, she'd somehow managed to slip away and get to sleep before him. And by morning, she'd left him in an empty bed.

No way would she pull any of that on him again.

"C'mon, boys," Warren announced. "Time to lend the missus a hand." He got up from the table. "Gotta do something to pay her back for this fine meal."

"Good idea," Jared said, getting up, too. "Better work off some of it before the dance starts."

They were heading in to town for the New Year's Eve festivities.

"You coming, boss?" Eddie asked.

Gabe saw Marissa turn to shoot him a look.

"Nope." He smiled slowly for her benefit. "My bride and I will be celebrating alone."

The boys made fast work of the drying, then went back to the bunkhouse to get ready.

Warren took his seat opposite Gabe again, setting down a plate of Marissa's pumpkin pie. Over his friend's shoulder, Gabe could see her puttering around at the sink.

After a good long while, she put the last dry dish away and moved to stand beside Warren. "You're sure you don't want to come in and watch the New Year's specials with us?"

Gabe glared, willing her to look him in the eye.

"No, thanks, Marissa," Warren said. "Haven't rung in the New Year's in a long time, and I'm too old to be thinking about it now. Besides, I'll appreciate the quiet with the boys all gone." He chuckled. "And I can sneak back in here for another piece of this pumpkin pie."

She smiled. "I left an extra slice on the counter just for you. Well." She paused, then finally met Gabe's eyes. "I'll see you over at the house."

"Sure enough." He gave her another slow smile and watched until she'd left the room. To her credit, she'd kept up pretenses in front of Warren. Later, he'd find some special way of thanking her for that.

"Hey, boss, sure you don't want to be heading out, too?"

The older man looked worried.

"You seem anxious to get rid of me, Warren."

"Heck, no, but the missus already left."

"She'll keep." Only eight o'clock. She sure wouldn't go off to bed at this early hour. "You know women," he added, "always wanting to get fancied up for a big event." He chuckled.

"Might not want to wait too long, boss."

Damn, first Doc and now Warren, both giving him advice—and neither of them even married.

He'd taken more than any man could stand with this arrangement with Marissa, and then some.

"You sure everything's okay?"

"Things're just fine, Warren." And they would be. Starting tonight.

Hell, they were legally married and living together, and now even sharing that big old bed. They might as well enjoy the benefits. He would take care of Marissa, could satisfy her and himself both, while keeping his heart intact.

No way, no how, would she make it to the bed before him tonight.

That's what he kept telling himself a while later, all the way across the yard to the house and up the stairs to the bedroom. He threw open the door and came to a dead halt in the doorway, staring in stunned disbelief.

Moonlight streaked through a crack between the curtains, illuminating Marissa on the bed with her eyes closed. The covers were bunched up under her chin, and the blanket rose and fell with her slow, steady breaths. She was asleep already.

Or playing possum.

He'd soon find out. He crossed the room and plopped onto the mattress.

She didn't blink an eye.

"Marissa?"

No answer. He swore under his breath and rested a hand on her shoulder.

"Sweetheart?"

Silence. He sighed. And reconsidered.

There was only one way out of this particular predicament.

He'd have to get her to feeling as eager as he was.

"WELL, THAT WAS one huge success, thanks to you." Sarah banged the cash-register drawer shut. "This was the busiest Saturday I've had in a long time."

Marissa laughed. Her cooking demonstration had gone very well, but she hadn't sold those books. "You're the saleswoman, Sarah."

"I've had those cookbooks for the past three years, and no one saw fit to buy them. Until today." She leaned against the counter. "Guess we'll be having another party here soon, won't we? A baby shower. Everyone's just tickled pink about the news. Or maybe tickled blue, since you don't know which yet." She laughed.

Marissa's heart gave a little lurch. "I'm really not that close to anyone here."

"You're Gabe's wife. That's good enough for Dillon. Marrying him makes you one of our own."

Marissa felt tears welling. How often had she dreamed about living in a community like this one?

How much longer would she be here?

Sarah peered at her. "All right, little mama. It's been a long day. Kick your feet up, and I'll go make tea."

Without protest, Marissa settled herself in one of the comfortable armchairs in Sarah's cozy reading nook.

All the while she'd been talking with Sarah, she had struggled to hold back a yawn. She was paying the price for the recent string of sleepless nights and early mornings.

She was paying the price of her deception.

By now, she had lost track of how many nights Doc's guests, a sweet older couple, had spent under their roof. Marissa barely knew the Josephsons were there. They had refused even to have a meal at the ranch.

"Oh, no," Mrs. Josephson had said gently. "We appreciate your putting us up and will only come back to sleep at night. We won't give you a bit of trouble."

Marissa could have groaned. Sweet Mrs. Josephson had no idea how much trouble they were causing her during the long, tension-filled nights they occupied her former bedroom, leaving her to share Gabe's room. And Gabe's bed.

Thank heaven, every night since their guests had arrived, her luck had held out. She had escaped to the bedroom before Gabe, then lain curled up under the covers when he arrived. Lord knows how she managed to keep up a calm, steady breathing when he entered the room. When he climbed into bed beside her. When, instead of pretending to be asleep, she yearned to move into his arms and nestle against his warmth.

Only, it wouldn't stop at that. She wouldn't be able to resist the sexual attraction she felt whenever he was near. The attraction that would draw her even closer.

The situation had led to nothing but agony and frustration—for both of them, she suspected.

She longed to turn back the clock and pretend none of this had happened.

Not the baby, of course. Never the baby.

She rested her hand on her stomach.

Overnight, it seemed, her body had changed. She wasn't yet ready for maternity clothes. Still, she could feel a tightness in her waistbands and, now, a gentle rounding beneath her hand.

She would never wish away this child she and Gabe had made.

She wanted only to wish away her guilt.

Miserable as she felt, she buried the fleeting thought about leaving the ranch, about leaving her troubles behind. Only a coward would run. Besides, she had to stay. She still had something to prove.

"You okay?"

She jumped. The sound of Gabe's deep drawl sent a rush of heat through her body. She had dreamed of him during the recent too-long nights. Had thought of him every waking moment. And now, apparently, had developed the ability to conjure him out of thin air.

Getting a grip on her emotions, she opened her eyes.

He perched on the edge of a flowered armchair opposite her, his feet planted wide and his elbows on his knees. He was focused on the hand she still had resting on her stomach.

"Yes, I'm fine," she said at last. "Just a little tired. What are you doing here?"

He shrugged. "Ran in for some extra twine. Thought I'd see how the talk went and make sure you got home okay."

The hardware store, yet again. "The demonstration went very well," she told him.

"Sure did."

Sarah had returned to the reading area, a cup and saucer in each hand.

"Tea, Gabe? That's the strongest I've got."

He shook his head.

"You should've strolled in a little bit ago. Marissa impressed every woman in the place. And their husbands will sure be happy when they get to taste some of the treats she shared."

"There are already a lot of happy husbands in Dillon, thanks to that candy-making lesson a week and a half ago."

"Including you, Miller?" Sarah demanded.

"Sure enough," he replied, meeting Marissa's gaze. "I'm the happiest husband of them all."

Marissa's breath caught.

It was different this time. He truly said the words as though he meant them. He hadn't added a fake endearment or tried to touch her, the way he usually did when he wanted to drive home the fact of their happy marriage. Could he really feel that way?

Her heart chose to believe his compliment was real.

And so was his concern, though he usually tried hard to hide it. He had come to town to escort her home. He'd said so.

She smiled at him.

No one had ever really cared for her, about her safety, this way. Of course, he could be worried because she was carrying his child. And she loved him for that. But she would allow herself to believe his attention meant he cared for her, too. He was making progress.

There was hope.

GABE FOLLOWED Marissa up the steps of Sarah's book-store. Her Mustang sat parked right outside the door, his pickup pulled up tight behind it.

He'd felt good earlier, when he'd found the car sitting there. Truth be told, maybe he hadn't needed that twine from the hardware store just yet. And maybe he hadn't needed to head back to the ranch by way of the book-store. But, as long as he'd been so close, it hadn't hurt to stop by. To offer to see Marissa home.

She stopped beside the Mustang and turned to look up at him, her eyes glowing. One long strand of hair trailed down the front of her coat. He couldn't keep from reaching out to touch it. For once, she didn't back away.

"Glad everything went okay," he muttered, wanting to keep her there so he could stare for a few more minutes.

"The group was wonderful," she told him. "In fact,

everyone in town has been nice about welcoming me here."

"Yeah. Now you've had some time to adjust, get to know people, you fit right in here in Dillon."

She did, too. Just as she fit right into his life. The thought both surprised and stunned him.

"Maybe," she said softly, "if I had met some of them the first time I was here, it would have made things a bit easier."

He frowned. "What was so hard about it?"

"It was…difficult, Gabe, with you out at work on the ranch all day. I mean, I knew that would happen, knew you wouldn't sit around holding my hand." She flushed and looked away. "I just didn't expect to be alone all day, with no one to talk with and nothing to do and to see you only for a couple hours a day. If I'd met more of the people from town the first time I lived on the ranch, I might not have felt so lonely."

"Lonely?"

"Well, of course. You were out of the house from before the sun rose until after it set. Mary kept to herself and refused to let me help with the cooking or cleaning. With my car still in Chicago, I had no way of getting in to town and nowhere to go when I got there."

She opened the car door and slid into the front seat.

He stared at her. For the second time, he felt stunned.

Maybe he was partly to blame. Coming from the big city, how could she have known what to expect from ranch life?

And maybe he'd made things worse by going back to his regular chores right after they'd got home from the honeymoon. Yet, to his mind, he'd put in the long hours, worked twice as hard in an effort to provide for her.

Only she hadn't seen it that way.

He reached down and touched her chin, turned her face to his. "Things are different this time around."

"Yes," she whispered. "Everything's different now."

And everything was.

He bent to wrap her coat around her. To protect her from the cold. But as he tucked the collar up under her chin, his hand brushed her cheek. Soft. Smooth.

Close.

He couldn't help himself. He had to lean toward her, had to touch her mouth with his. He did, and she responded.

It was over faster than blinking.

A moment later, he was closing the door, keeping her safe, climbing into his pickup to follow her home.

And thinking about that kiss. Light and sweet and very short-lived. But still downright erotic.

Maybe, for him and Marissa, it couldn't be any other way.

He wanted the chance to find out. Yet he couldn't risk giving his heart to her. Trusting her not to run off with it.

And in a sudden rush of understanding, he knew he wanted her happy. He wanted things to work out. Not just so the baby could inherit his ranch. Not only for someone to share his bed.

But because he wanted her to stay.

THE HOUSE SEEMED quieter than normal as Marissa finished brushing her teeth. She looked in the mirror, saw the dark rings beneath her eyes and grimaced.

Though she had been going to bed earlier each night mostly to avoid Gabe, she had been even more tired than usual lately. Last night, she had wanted to stay awake long enough to talk to him. To continue the feeling of closeness that had begun outside The Book Cellar. She curled up on the living-room couch, waiting—and had awoken this morning, swaddled in a soft blue blanket.

Gabe, when pressed, admitted he had come in from the bunkhouse, found her fast asleep and tucked her in.

She sighed. Maybe she actually needed that extra sleep. But it was a missed opportunity to talk with him.

And today, they hadn't had a moment alone.

How ironic—all those days she'd wanted to avoid Gabe, and now the one time she wanted him to herself, she hadn't a chance.

Even tonight, after they finished supper in the bunk-house, she had hoped he would return to the main house with her. Instead, he settled down with Warren and a stack of catalogs on cattle care. Not the cozy, private talk she had looked forward to after their mutual under-standing the day before.

She lingered. Stalled. And finally asked Gabe outright if he planned to return to the house with her.

"You go ahead, honey," he said. "Warren and I've got some business to take care of."

"Boss, it can wait—" Warren began.

"That's all right." Gabe smiled at her.

So, considering she couldn't add much to the topic of cattle disease, she left.

An hour passed, then two. When even a second cup of tea couldn't stop her eyelids from drooping, she had headed upstairs, leaving on the light above the kitchen sink for Gabe.

And taking with her a guilty secret.

Earlier that afternoon, the Josephsons had left, after thanking Marissa for her hospitality. And when Gabe came home, she didn't tell him.

The guest bedroom was empty. She could move back downstairs again. But—another irony—just as she hadn't been ready to share a room with Gabe, now she wasn't ready to leave.

In the bathroom mirror, she saw her cheeks flame.

She wanted the sweetness of their kiss again. And yet she feared the sizzle beneath it.

Instead, she would settle for just one more night beside him, just one more morning of waking before he did, of seeing his dark hair against the pillow and his face softened in sleep.

Was that too much to ask?

Afraid of what her own answer might be, she hung her robe on the bathroom door, flipped off the light switch and escaped.

With a sigh, she entered the bedroom. The dresser lamp she had left on low gave her plenty of light.

More than enough to see Gabe, propped up on one elbow on his side of the bed.

"Gabe." She gulped and clutched at her nightgown,

wishing now she hadn't removed the robe. "I didn't know you were here."

"Came in quiet, in case you were sleeping."

"Oh…" She had wanted the chance to talk with him tonight. She just hadn't expected their conversation to take place in the bedroom. Hadn't expected to share a bed with him at a time she couldn't pretend to be asleep.

Gabe relaxed in slumber was one thing; Gabe awake beside her was too dangerous to contemplate.

Frantically, she searched for a graceful way to leave. For a logical excuse to return downstairs. For anything that would get her—or *him*—out of the room.

"Um…the bathroom's all yours."

"Showered up in the bunkhouse. All ready for bed?" He tapped her side of the mattress. "Got it all toasty for you."

She hesitated.

"C'mon, Marissa. You must be tired, all that extra cooking you've been doing over the holidays."

"No, not really."

"Well, c'mon, anyway. I won't bite." He chuckled. "Ate so much Sunday supper, I won't be looking for food for a while."

If the way to a man's heart was through his stomach, then maybe she'd had the key to unlock Gabe's emotions all along. Too bad she couldn't whip out a tempting treat right now to distract him.

Steps dragging, she approached the bed. Gabe watched her every move.

Fingers trembling, she plucked at the plaid comforter, barely making a ripple in the fabric. Gabe swept his arm across the bed, pulling the comforter and sheet back invitingly.

She caught her breath at the sight his movement exposed. Hunter-green flannel pajama bottoms, cupped low around his hips. Dark hair that started as a narrow column near his waist, then widened as it rose to feather across his muscled chest. Heat radiated from the bed. She could almost feel it reaching out to her and ached to let the warmth pull her in.

"C'mon," he said again. "It's about time we got this new year off to the right start."

In spite of her longing, his words made her stiffen. Sex wasn't what she wanted or needed from Gabe right now.

He saw her reaction and frowned. "I'm talking about sleeping together, that's all. Sharing a bed. You wanted to be partners, didn't you?"

"Yes," she whispered. Reluctantly.

"Then, come to bed. Let's just talk."

With more than a little trepidation, she kicked off her bedroom slippers and climbed onto the bed. Gabe lifted his arm, tenting the sheet and comforter over her, enveloping her in the soft fabric and cozy warmth. She grasped the bedclothes close to her and tried to get comfortable. Tried to keep from instinctively gravitating toward him.

Tried to keep her body from betraying her.

If Gabe felt disappointed that she didn't snuggle near, he didn't let himself show it. Instead, he tucked the covers up under her chin, the way he had tucked her coat collar around her the day before. The way he must have tucked in the blue blanket last night. With that tenderness he tried so hard to hide.

Between them on the comforter, he rested a big, careworn hand that could thrill her with the merest brush. One that could cherish her, too. How gently he had touched her face as she sat in her car outside Sarah's bookstore. How carefully he had settled the seat belt around her.

She could imagine those big, gentle hands holding their child. The image made her heart swell with such tenderness her ribs ached.

"You like it here?" Gabe said suddenly. "Dillon, I mean?"

She knew he was picking up the conversation they had started yesterday. She knew she had to tell him the truth.

"Yes, I like it here. When I was little," she confessed, "I always dreamed about having a big family and living in a small town, where everyone knew everyone else."

"Not what you had, growing up."

"No, not at all."

The sympathy in his tone touched her and gave her renewed hope. If he could listen and understand, maybe he could learn to share. From that, they could forge a real friendship.

Her own life would have been so much better if her parents hadn't been bitter enemies, if her mother hadn't been the kind of woman she was. She wanted that better life for her baby.

Just as she wanted this marriage to be real.

The thought stole her breath. For a moment, she couldn't move, couldn't think and couldn't hear Gabe's voice, until his sudden emphasis told her she had missed something.

"But you're here now. In Dillon."

"I'm here," she agreed. "Gabe…"

She had an appointment with Doc the next afternoon.

She hesitated to mention it, knowing how Gabe had reacted when she'd first told him about the appointment. Knowing he would recall again another three-week anniversary. The three weeks they had been married, when she left him.

But she wanted him to visit the doctor with her, to share with her, as a real husband would.

"Tomorrow…I'm going into Doc's for an ultrasound. I'd like you to come, too." She waited, her heart pounding.

"I'll be there," he murmured.

They lay in silence. Gradually, her heartbeat slowed.

After a while, he spoke again in the same soft tone. "One thing I've wanted to find out, since Christmas Day at Mrs. G's."

"What?"

"Something Kevin never got around to asking you. What was your best Christmas ever?"

She turned her head to look into his light brown eyes, then glanced away, afraid her own eyes might reveal too much. But, as with his question about how she felt being in Dillon, she had to answer him truthfully.

"This one," she whispered. "This was the best Christmas ever."

He reached out a hand to brush her cheek with his fingers. Instead of her usual, electric response to his touch, a slow, satisfying warmth seeped into her skin and flowed through her body in waves that matched the calm rhythm of her heart, beat for beat.

He followed his fingers with his lips, leaving a trail of kisses down her cheek, across her jaw and, finally, finding her mouth with his. He was searching, thorough, but oh so gentle, teasing a response from her lips. From her body.

When he reached for her, she went willingly, gladly, longing to relive the closeness of the first time they had made love. Of the night, she was certain, they had conceived their child.

When he touched her wordlessly, she answered the same way, letting her eyes and body tell him what she felt too shy to say. That this was what she had longed for, in those few short weeks she had spent with him, and during those many long weeks they had spent apart. This was what she wanted. What she needed.

What she'd found in her heart when she'd met him.

This savoring of being together. This slow taking of pleasure.

This celebration of love.

Chapter Sixteen

Silently, Marissa crept down the stairs and into the kitchen. The cold glare from the light over the sink greeted her. That light had seemed so welcoming earlier, when she'd left it on for Gabe. When she had foolishly imagined it leading him home to her.

Sinking into a chair, she pulled her robe closer around her, still feeling the warmth of his bed, still tingling from his sure touch, his knowing hands. But not from his loving embrace.

Not once had he held her to him during their love-making—

No. She couldn't call it that.

Only moments later, he had turned onto his side, facing away from her, and fallen deeply asleep. No repeat performance or two, as there had always been during the nights of their honeymoon. No holding her close until she drifted to sleep. No time to linger for pillow talk…although Marissa had always done most of the talking.

Gabe had had sex. He had satisfied himself, gotten what he'd wanted and gone serenely to sleep, while she had lain awake, hot tears of shame soaking her pillow.

Because Gabe wasn't the only one at fault.

She had gone to him willingly, giving in to him, showing once again that she had no willpower where he was concerned.

Proving Father right. She *was* no better than her mother.

She crossed her arms on the tabletop and shoved her hands into the sleeves of her robe, trying to warm them. Trying to push away old memories. Still, they came....

Four days after meeting Gabe, that night at the show, she was still living in a magical world with him.

They avoided the fancy restaurants, gaudy casinos, risqué shows. Instead, they ate at open-air Western barbecues and local Mexican restaurants. He taught her to two-step at a country dance hall. They took a stagecoach ride in the desert, in a town so far from Las Vegas the bright lights of the city couldn't dim the sky full of stars.

He gave her gifts she'd never had before. Candy made from prickly-pear cactus. A balloon in the shape of Nevada. Someone who listened when she talked about her dreams.

And something else.

"I'm thinking we ought to try out one of those wedding chapels," he told her as her week in Las Vegas came to an end.

"One without an Elvis impersonator, I presume?"

"You got that right."

She smiled. "Is this another proposition, cowboy?"

"No, Marissa, it's not." He put a forefinger under her chin and tilted her face up to his. "It's a proposal."

A proposal she eagerly accepted…

Just as, tonight, she had eagerly accepted his invitation into his bed. She had responded to her overwhelming desire to feel loved and cherished and wanted.

And she had given in to her lust.

The last thought hit like a slap of ice-cold water. She put her head down on her crossed arms, trying to fight off the resulting sting of tears.

When would she finally come to terms with the truth?

The fantasy was over. The fairy tale had ended. The magic had disappeared in the face of real life.

GABE WALKED INTO DOC'S waiting area the next afternoon, spotted Marissa on the other side of the room, and froze in his tracks.

His mind flashed back to the night before.

Then, his thoughts and hands and body had been focused on only one thing.

Today, he'd looked back without those sexual urges driving him.

Today, he'd closed his eyes and seen Marissa naked beside him, noted what he hadn't taken time to register. The little differences in her body, brought on from carrying a child. The heavier feel of her breasts. The thickening around her middle. The new shape of her belly, the soft roundness she hadn't had there before.

He took a deep breath and nearly crushed his Stetson in one hand.

When Marissa looked up and saw him coming, her eyes widened. He smiled and slid into the chair beside hers.

"Guess you forgot I said I'd join you this afternoon." It took a powerful effort to keep his voice level. And his hands to himself. He rested the battered Stetson on one knee.

"You really didn't need to come with me today, after all. It's just a routine ultrasound."

"No problem," he said, notching his voice down a bit, mindful of Doc's nurse standing a few feet from them in the reception area. "This is what daddies do, isn't it?"

She looked away, but not before he saw the sheen of tears filling her eyes. He reached for her hand.

Gladys came up to them, her white shoes silent on the carpet. "We're ready for you."

He leaned closer to Marissa. "I'll give you and Doc some privacy for the examination," he said gruffly, "but I'll be waiting here when it's time for the next step."

He squeezed his wife's motionless hand, then released it.

As she moved through the doorway to Doc's examining rooms, he sat back and took stock of what had happened last night.

Yep, making love with Marissa had been the best thing. It had reinforced the wisdom of his plan. He'd gotten close to her, given her what she wanted—what he wanted, too, if he had to confess it.

All without risking his heart.

He thought hard about what she'd told him a couple

days ago. How she'd felt when he'd first brought her to the ranch.

Now that he knew what had gone wrong the first time, he had the power to fix things. And he would. He'd keep her happy, just like he did last night. Keep her here in Dillon, on his ranch, where his child belonged.

Gladys appeared in the doorway. "Your turn, Gabe."

He followed her down the hall. "I know the way, Gladys. You know, I've visited this office all my life. Checkups. Vaccinations. Once in a while, some stitches."

"But never for the reason you've come here today."

"True enough." For a minute, his step faltered.

Gladys opened the door to Doc's examination room, gave him a friendly pat on the shoulder, then left.

Gabe looked across the room.

Marissa sat on a long leather table, a paper sheet draped across her lap. In the background were a couple of machines he had never seen before. Never had need to, till now.

"Well, looks like we've got all the interested parties on hand." Doc adjusted the stethoscope around his neck. "You both ready to take a look at your little one?"

"Yes."

"You bet."

Doc had Marissa adjust herself the way he needed, did whatever he had to with his instruments and the small machine on the rolling cart.

Gabe crossed the room and took his wife's hand in his.

At the press of a switch, the machine's dark screen crackled to life.

A moment later, the black rectangle turned gray-white with the fuzzy image of the inside of his wife's womb. Their hands tightened around each other. The screen blurred, and he blinked his eyes a few times, waiting for the picture to clear.

Suddenly, he saw the image on the screen flicker. He heard his own gasp, matched by Marissa's soft exclamation. He saw the outline of a head, a shoulder—a body.

His breath caught tight in his chest.

The outline moved.

His insides shook. He gripped Marissa's hand tighter.

"Active little tyke," Doc said in a low voice. "Want to know what you've got here?"

"Yes," Gabe and Marissa said together.

Gabe stared, fascinated, as the image…as the baby shifted.

"Well," Doc said. "Looks like you have yourselves a son."

A son.

He thought again of the soft roundness of Marissa's belly, the slight curve that just fit the palm of his hand.

That was his son, brought to life inside her.

The rest of the visit passed in a blur. He knew Doc gave Marissa instructions, knew he himself helped her from the examining table, waited till she'd finished dressing and then escorted her down the hall. He knew he walked her outside, helped her into the Mustang, shut the door behind her.

And then a wave of emotion hit him so strong it near knocked him off his feet.

Up till that moment in Doc's office, "baby" had been a concept. An event that wouldn't come to pass for a while. A reason to keep Marissa here. An heir to inherit his ranch.

Now he knew all that had just been words. None of them really mattered.

Because now that baby was living and breathing and truly his.

The thought left him spinning.

He sucked in a deep breath and braced his hands on the side of his pickup. He blinked hard and shook his head to clear his vision. He made himself a solemn vow.

He'd do whatever it took to keep the mother of his child happy.

Because he was damn well going to raise his son.

WHEN HE MET Marissa in the ranch yard after driving home in their separate vehicles, she stayed quiet. Too quiet.

It worried him as he went to the bunkhouse to change into his work clothes.

It worried him on his way to the barn to saddle up Sunrise.

Halfway along, he stopped in his tracks to retrace his steps to the main house.

There, nothing moved. Nothing made a sound except his boots thumping as he walked through the empty rooms, and his pulse pounding in his ears.

He didn't know much about women. The past had

taught him that. So had his experiences with Marissa up to now. Dumb as a fence post he might be, but he could still tell in his gut when something wasn't right.

He found her upstairs, fast asleep in his bed.

One notch at a time, his pulse came down. He thought long and hard for a moment, trying to figure things out.

She needed rest for carrying his baby. Or the night before had tired her out. Sure, one of those reasons would explain her unnatural silence, her quick retreat. Wouldn't it?

He left the room, taking extra care to be quiet with his boots on the stairs.

And taking a powerful load of dread right along with him.

As he headed out to the barn again, clouds rolled in, dark and brooding as his mood. He stomped through the open doorway.

Warren looked up from the feed pen he'd been filling.

"What's going on, Gabe?" he asked. Using his name was a dead giveaway. Warren knew something was up.

So Gabe just blurted it out. "I saw my son today."

"Dang."

Warren never cussed.

"Yeah," Gabe agreed. He took a deep breath. "Closest thing to a miracle I've ever seen."

"A boy, huh?"

"My son."

"Dang," Warren said again. "Double dang." He

slapped Gabe on the back nearly hard enough to send him flying.

Gabe laughed.

All the rest of that afternoon, his hands moved, but his mind strayed four hundred acres away.

It didn't make sense for Marissa to be so close-mouthed after seeing the baby.

Of course, the sight had staggered him. And he'd kept his reactions to himself. Natural enough, for a man. But a woman would've acted differently. Would she not?

The temperature dropped and the sky got darker, and so did the feelings churning his insides.

BY LATE AFTERNOON, Gabe quit fighting himself. He gave Sunrise her head, let her take him home. Had to, because his mind wasn't on the ranch, but back at the house with Marissa.

He turned the reins over to Warren, and the old cowboy's face deepened in wrinkles. "What's wrong?"

"I don't know. Something's worrying Marissa."

"Not surprising. Carrying a baby, she's bound to be a bit touchy. She just needs some extra attention, is all."

He nearly laughed aloud. Warren had less experience with women than he did, yet he seemed eager enough to impart his wisdom.

At this point, he'd take the man's advice. And Doc's.

"That's why I headed in early. Thought I'd surprise her with an invitation to supper out."

"Good idea."

Yeah, a nice meal would do the trick. Not Delia's. Someplace out of town. Fancy. Someplace a professional chef would find worthy. They'd have to go a few miles to find a restaurant like that.

He'd drive all night, if need be.

He stopped first at the bunkhouse, showered, grabbed a bottle of the aftershave he kept stowed away in the corner cabinet. The same bottle he'd taken to Vegas with him. The kind Marissa said she couldn't get enough of.

He gave a final pat to his jaws, grinned at himself in the mirror and left, whistling.

Inside the house, he looked around the kitchen. No sign here of Marissa getting supper ready. None in the bunkhouse, either. Just as well. Warren and the boys would be chowing down at Delia's this evening, for the first time since Marissa had come back. She sure had spoiled them.

And that's just what he planned to do for her.

Get her so spoiled, so comfortable, so happy, she'd never want to leave Dillon. Or the ranch. Or him.

A wave of uneasiness hit him. He pushed it away.

"Hey, Marissa!"

No answer.

He strode across the kitchen and clomped up the hall stairs, calling her name again. Still no answer.

That gave him pause.

Of course. She'd been sleeping like a baby when he'd left the house earlier. She probably still lay curled up under the covers.

He turned on his heel and went to the bedroom.

The bed was empty, sheet tucked in, comforter squared off and without a wrinkle. As if she had never slept there.

His heart skipped a beat.

He checked the closet, the bathroom, the hallway again.

"Marissa," he yelled.

Still no answer.

Maybe she'd gone up to the attic for something and hadn't heard him call. He climbed another set of stairs, stood staring at the dust motes tumbling in the streak of light from a window. Stood worrying at something he'd seen—or hadn't seen—since he'd come back into the house. Besides Marissa.

A sudden thought sent him down the two flights of stairs, across the hall and into the kitchen, then out the back door.

Sure enough. His pickup sat in the driveway. The spot beside it, where she always parked, sat empty.

He inhaled a breath of cold air.

Maybe she'd run in to town with an order for Delia. To pick up some extra groceries. For a visit with Sarah.

But he shook his head.

It was something more than that. He could feel it in his bones. He could tell by how his gut churned, by the way his hands had started to sweat. Now he recalled what had hit him upstairs, recollected that worry about something being just not right.

A stab of suspicion told him what that something was.

This time, his trip through the house took ten times

longer than it'd ever taken in his life. This time, he didn't want to get where he was going. Didn't want to find what he knew he would.

He pushed himself through the motions. A slow, reluctant progression from kitchen to hallway. One dragging step after another up the stairs. A loose-limbed stumble along the hall to his bedroom.

As if he'd forgotten how to walk.

As if he'd never known how.

He stood frozen a long time looking into the room, not stepping through the doorway, just watching the light from the west-facing window change as the afternoon wore on.

He felt older than the Texas soil his house stood upon. Worn out by the unwanted memories pressing him down.

Finally, when he could take it no longer, he shuffled across the room to the closet.

Fading daylight trickled into the enclosed space, lighting the bare area in one corner. Showing him what he didn't want to see. Confirming what he'd known all along would happen.

When she'd learned about Doc's guests coming to visit, she'd had him cart everything of hers from the guest room up to his bedroom. She'd emptied the suitcases and stacked them neatly in the corner of the closet. Now, that corner was empty. The suitcases were gone.

He didn't want to believe it.

He'd wanted Marissa to be different.

Vainly, he sought for something to prove his certainty wrong.

Instead, everywhere he looked, he found something to taunt him. Clothes hangers dangling. Shoe racks gaping. Dresser top gleaming, her hairbrush and comb gone.

He stumbled across to the bathroom. No pink toothbrush in the plastic holder. No toothpaste tube on the shelf. No soft bathrobe hanging from the hook on the door.

There it was. More proof than any man could ever need. More proof than he ever wanted.

And no way to escape the truth.

Marissa had left him.

Chapter Seventeen

As Marissa pulled into the ranch yard, the sun again slipped behind a dark cloud. She shivered, fighting both a sudden chill and an overwhelming sense of fatigue and hopelessness.

The nap she had pretended to take earlier in an attempt to avoid Gabe had turned into a genuine, if fitful, sleep. Yet the short rest hadn't helped her, not her body or her mind or her emotions, one bit.

How could it, when her own body and mind, her own ragged emotions, had caused her to betray herself?

She still felt shamed by her actions of the evening before.

Still felt shaken by that afternoon's visit to Doc.

A tremor had coursed through her when she first saw the baby. Their son. The same tremor had shot through Gabe, too, in a rush of unbridled emotion she felt in his hand clamped tight around hers. Saw in his awestruck expression. Heard in his gasped breath. All undeniable signs of something he would steadfastly refuse to share. Probably even refuse to admit.

She hadn't bothered trying to ask him anything.

Shivering again, she climbed from the car. After a long, deep breath of cold air, she trudged up the back steps and opened the door to the kitchen.

A glance at the clock over the stove told her she had plenty of time to get supper ready for Gabe and Warren and the boys.

Funny, how easily she had slipped into the language of the ranch this time around, as she never had before. Her formal Chicago evening dinner had become "supper." Gabe's men had become "the boys." She felt a part of life on the ranch now, a part of Dillon.

A part of everything except Gabe's heart.

As she closed the door behind her, he burst into the room.

"Where the hell are you going?"

Shock froze her fingers on the top button of her coat.

He stood staring at her, his eyes wide, his hands fisted, his chest heaving.

She forced her fingers to move. "I'm not going anywhere," she said, as calmly as she could.

"Sure." He curled his lip in disbelief. Or disgust.

"What's wrong, Gabe?"

"Everything's fine. The way I expected. Just took longer than I thought for you to decide to get the hell out of here."

The pain behind his words gave her a sad kind of

comfort. It made a difference to him, whether or not she was around, no matter how hard he fought to deny it.

"So that's it. You noticed I moved my clothes from the bedroom."

"Clothes and suitcases, too."

"Yes. The Josephsons left. Yesterday, as a matter of fact. So I brought everything of mine back to the guest bedroom."

"Yeah, right. You weren't in the house at all. What happened, get halfway to town and realize you forgot something?"

She winced at the accusing tone, wanted to snap back at him, but stopped herself. Though this wasn't the emotion she had hoped to see, at least he was sharing something. And there was more than just anger behind his tirade. "I went to visit Sarah."

"Where's the Mustang—out front where I wouldn't see it, coming in the back trail?"

"It's right next to your truck."

"All ready for a quick getaway?"

Against the steady stream of his sarcasm, her patience began to wear thin. "You're not listening to me, Gabe. Or you're not hearing me, one or the other." She threw the back door open again. "Look. The car is right there."

His focus slid past her to the door, but he refused to move.

She shook her head. "This isn't just about my leaving the bedroom, is it? You thought I'd left for good."

He stayed silent.

"You should know I wouldn't do that, at least not without telling you first."

"Like last time?"

She thought of when she had left, of the things she had tried before leaving. Those few short months ago, she'd seen how obstinate Gabe could be. She'd broken her heart in the struggle to break down the wall that stood between them. An impossible task back then.

Now, she didn't know if she could muster the strength to try again, when Gabe obviously hadn't changed at all. But this could be the last chance she would have to fight for what she wanted. She had to try. For the baby's sake. And for her own.

"Things were different last time," she began. "We didn't have a child to consider. And even then, I left you a note."

"Note or not, doesn't matter. You're all the same."

All?

That one word pierced her heart.

How many people had hurt Gabe in the past, leaving him so wary of forming a commitment? Leaving him so resistant to accepting love?

Slowly, she closed the door and hung her coat on its usual peg. She took the very seat she had occupied the morning of her return to the ranch. So much had gone on in these few short weeks.

And, clearly, so much had yet to happen.

She thought back to those bits of personal information Gabe had seen fit to reveal to her. Another drawback to marrying quickly, without getting to know him first.

"You said to me once that women don't stay on this ranch. I thought you meant your mother, and then me. The two of us. But, just now, you said 'all.'"

He remained silent.

Tears of frustration prickled behind her eyelids. "We're back where we started months ago. How can I understand, if you won't open up to me?"

He looked away.

"You just said 'You're all the same.'" She forced a teasing note into her tone. "Just how many wives have you had, anyway?"

"The grapevine didn't tell you that, too?"

Her patience snapped. So did she. "If it did, would I be asking?" A sinking feeling in the pit of her stomach made her wish she'd held back the words. She'd never thought about other women in Gabe's life. She had wanted to be the only one.

He crossed his arms over his chest. "I was engaged once before. Girl grew up here. You'd think *she'd* stick around a small town, wouldn't you?"

"What happened?"

"She got bored. Wanted more. Took off for the big city. Here one day, gone the next. Just like my mother."

"And just like me?"

He said nothing.

"They were behind all your references to the big city, weren't they? And all those times you called me a 'city gal'?" She took a deep breath, hoping to control her dismay. It didn't work. "How could you still compare me to them, Gabe, with what I told you last night about always wanting to live in a small town?"

"You lived here. And left."

"It's not the same." She leaned forward, gripping the edge of the table. "They left and never came back. But I *did.* You can't hold me up against them."

He didn't answer.

"When I left, it wasn't because I wanted to live in a big city. It was because we weren't working together, we weren't a team." She sighed. "If you would just give me the tiniest encouragement—"

"That courting stuff again? Is that all you want from me?"

Her breath caught so sharply, her chest ached. "That's so unfair, Gabe. That's not what I asked from you, not before I left and not when I first came back again. And you know it." She paused, waited and went on. "I wanted you to open up to me. To be equal partners. That's all I've ever wanted."

A sudden thought hit her. She raised her hand to her mouth, holding back a cry of anguish, steadying herself for what she needed to say.

"You don't trust me, do you?" This time, she didn't wait for a reply that would never come. "The first day I went shopping in town, you insisted on going with me. When I did the talk at Sarah's bookstore, you showed up unannounced. Even this afternoon, coming to town for my appointment with Doc…"

He said nothing.

She laughed, a strangled sound without humor. "I could understand if only you'd done all that to play your part of my loving husband. To stick to our agreement. Instead, you were keeping an eye on me, making sure I wouldn't run away. Or maybe you were sure I would and just wanted to confirm it."

Again, he refused to respond.

She pushed herself to her feet and had to brace her hands on the table for a moment to stop her trembling. Then she slowly crossed the room to stand in front of him. Waited until his gaze met hers.

"I thought you did all that out of concern for me and the baby." Her voice broke. She fought a rush of tears. "I wanted to believe it, Gabe. I wanted to think you love me. Because I love you."

She rested her hand on his arm, needing to touch him. Desperate to reach him.

He stared at her, unblinking, his jaw set and his body rigid. He didn't respond, but his body spoke for him. Corded muscle tensed beneath her palm.

She had done her best to get through to him and, again, she had failed.

She had declared her love for him and been rejected.

Dropping her hand, she stepped back.

"I think it would be best if I move into town until we sort things out."

MARISSA TOOK one last look around the guest room.

No, she hadn't forgotten anything. In fact, she hadn't had much to pack. Most of her suitcases were already filled—untidily, because she had flung things into the bags earlier that day in her haste to clear every trace of herself from Gabe's bedroom.

She wanted no reminders of giving herself, eagerly and willingly, to a man who didn't love her.

Who would never love her.

Not because he was cold or hard inside, but because he had been hurt before and would do whatever he could to protect his heart.

She, knowing nothing of this, had done exactly the wrong thing and had lost any chance she might have had with him, when she left so soon after their honeymoon.

Today, the partially packed bags had made it easier for her to move back to the guest room.

But when it came to moving out, to leaving Gabe completely, nothing could make things easier. Nothing could take away the pain she'd felt as she stood in the kitchen, her heart breaking, faced with his accusations. His silences. His stony refusals to communicate.

Nothing could ease her sorrow as, at last, she understood.

All along, she had been fooling herself, believing she was willing to endure the lonely ranch life for her baby's sake. Convinced she'd given in to lust. Now, alone in the room she was about to leave, maybe forever, she had to admit the truth.

She had loved Gabe from the beginning and loved him even more now. She truly wanted to be his wife.

Unfortunately, all these realizations had come too late.

He might want to be a real father, but he would never be able to trust her—or any woman—enough to become a real husband.

And that's what she wanted and needed in her life.

She lifted her smallest suitcase, wrapped her arms around it, as if it could shield her breaking heart.

Though she ached to make her life with him, it would hurt so much worse to stay when he didn't want her— and when she had brought it all on herself.

She picked up her suitcases and went out into the hall, hoping she could leave the house without having to face Gabe again. The coward's way out, maybe, but she would take it.

He didn't give her that option.

He stood at the bottom of the stairs, his hands shoved into his jeans pockets. "Running away again, Marissa?"

He'd said that to her before, and this time, she didn't have the strength to argue. "Only as far as town, as I told you," she said as steadily as she could. She eased down the stairs as steadily as possible, too, refusing to let him see any sign of weakness from her. Her head held high, she walked past him.

"You can stay here, if you want to."

The words jerked her to a halt. Her body trembled in a rush of hopefulness and anticipation. She stood unmoving, praying, as Gabe went on.

"You can move back into the guest room. And stay there. We can raise the child together. Keep our lives apart."

She remained still, barely breathing, needing a moment to find her voice. Wanting to weep at his dry, unemotional offer, when she craved so much more.

Finally, she found the strength to turn back to him. "The situation hasn't changed from what it was when I first left, Gabe. You haven't changed. But I have. For me, our original agreement isn't enough." Her voice sounded much steadier, her words much more determined than she had expected. Both rang with the conviction of what she now truly believed.

Despite that, she couldn't leave without giving him one last chance. Giving herself one more try to see if he had really hardened his heart to her.

"I'm not going to accept a one-way commitment, Gabe. I want a real marriage, in every respect. You can be a father to our child. You *are* our baby's father. But I can't accept what you're offering. Because what I need—what we both need—is a full, loving relationship. And I won't cheat either of us out of it."

He didn't respond.

She tightened her grip on her suitcases and blinked away tears. This time, she couldn't keep her voice from trembling. "I have to go now, Gabe."

He looked at her, his eyes dark and intense, filled with an emotion she couldn't name. An emotion he wouldn't acknowledge.

And she knew their relationship, such as it was, such as it ever had been, was over.

NOT KNOWING where else to go, Marissa had fled to The Book Cellar.

Sarah had taken one look at her face and gone to put the Closed sign on the front door.

"I don't know what to do now," Marissa confessed as she accepted the cup of tea Sarah held out to her.

In all the years of moving from city to city with her mother, she had learned not to get too close to people, because she wouldn't be around very long. In the years since, with her father, she had spent more time studying than socializing.

Sarah Jones was the closest thing to a best friend Marissa had ever had.

She unburdened herself, telling Sarah about her history and her heartbreak, all in a torrent of jumbled words.

Finally, exhausted mentally, physically and emotionally, she took a sip of her tea. Oddly enough, the still-hot brew seemed to calm her. Or maybe it was Sarah's soothing presence.

"I know he cares about me and the baby, Sarah. He offered to paint the baby's room—insisted on it, really, even though he could have kept away. And when we were at Doc's office, and he saw the ultrasound…" She swallowed hard and repeated fiercely, "I know he cares. But he won't let himself love us, because of what I did." She shook her head. "Maybe the next woman he meets won't make the same mistakes. Maybe he'll be able to love her *and* trust her."

"Marissa, that man's issues with trust won't be resolved in the next minute. And they began long before you met him."

"I know, but I'm to blame for how he feels now."

"No. He's to blame, for being pigheaded enough not to see what he's got right in front of him. And I'm not meaning that just about you."

"His fiancée?"

Brows raised in surprise, Sarah nodded.

"He told me about her. Finally. Today."

"I can't honestly speak about his mother, because she's been gone so long I barely remember her. But his fiancée—"

She paused, and Marissa didn't want to push her. This unplanned pity party was bad enough, without having it degenerate into a gossip fest. Dillon already had a big enough grapevine, as Gabe had told her.

Yet it certainly hadn't spread the news to her about a fiancée. He had stunned her completely when he'd told her. Her heart still ached from the news. Not with jealousy, as she might have expected, but envy.

Had he willingly courted that other woman, without her having to demand it? Had he loved her, before she left him and went away? Had he trusted her, as he never had Marissa?

The last thought stole her breath, hitting her with a bitter truth she hadn't understood until that moment.

"I thought he didn't trust me now, because I had left him once before. But he never trusted me at all, Sarah. Not even when we first came to the ranch after we were married. From the very beginning, he never thought I would stay. He never even gave me a chance."

"That's likely true. After his mama left, and then years later, that other one… Well, let's just say he didn't use the brains he'd been born with when he hooked up with her. She was nice enough, but not meant for him. And not meant to be a ranch wife, either."

"Neither am I."

Sarah's eyes narrowed. "I'm thinking that's not the real Marissa talking."

In spite of her predicament, she found one corner of her mouth curling in a smile.

No, that wasn't the real Marissa Miller talking. Not anymore. Not now that she knew exactly what she wanted. And, as she had told Gabe such a short while ago, what she deserved.

"You're right," she agreed. "But you have to admit, I *did* hurt him when I left him so soon after we were married."

"Sure, you did. There's no getting around that. But he'd have been hurt no matter when you'd gone. And from what you've just been telling me, he's got to shoulder some of the blame."

"I suppose so. The fact is, I did it, and now I have to face the consequences." She set her teacup down on the edge of Sarah's big oak desk. She had made another decision. "May I use your telephone?"

Sarah looked apprehensive. "Don't you think you both might need some more time…?"

Marissa shook her head. "Don't worry. It's not Gabe I'm calling. It's another man I need to stand up to." She surprised herself by laughing aloud at Sarah's expression.

If she could laugh, she could survive. She could do whatever she needed to do.

Gently, she swatted her friend's arm. "I'm talking about my father."

"Oh." Sarah nodded. "In that case, I'd best go back to dusting my bookshelves."

Left alone in the privacy of the small office, Marissa dialed the long-distance number of her father's New York headquarters. He would be back from Europe by now. His cool voice would come through the telephone receiver—after she had gone through a series of secretaries and assistants, of course.

His cold tone would never bother her again. No matter how much he thought she was like her mother, she was also her father's daughter. She could be as cold and precise as he could. And she was strong enough now to stand up to him.

After all, she had been strong enough today to do the right thing.

To leave another man who didn't love her.

Chapter Eighteen

Gabe stood in the dimly lit hallway after a hard day driving himself on the ranch. Trying to outrun Marissa. Trying to forget he ever had a wife.

It didn't work.

Thoughts of her had kept him company through the long hours of the night. Had ridden along with him out on the ranch every minute of the day. Were with him now, in this house she'd left the day before, taking a part of him with her. Yet when she'd told him she was going, he couldn't bring himself to beg her to stay.

He brushed his fingers against the pine bough she'd twisted around the stair rail. Saw the wreath hanging on the wall. Couldn't stop himself from looking into the living room.

He saw the small pair of cowboy boots he'd brought down from the box in his old room, dusted off and set on the coffee table.

But he also saw Marissa there. Curled up on the couch the night he'd come in to seal their bargain.

Carrying a tray of hot chocolate and cookies. Sitting beside him, her eyes glowing from the lights on the Christmas tree.

That blasted tree.

He'd sat in front of it last night like some seven-year-old waiting for Santa. But the tree stayed dark, and whatever he might've hoped for never happened.

He backed away from the door.

Down the hall, he stopped in the guest room doorway. It had never crossed his mind to check that room yesterday. He'd had no idea the Josephsons had left.

And now all he could see was Marissa standing there, her hands filled with silky bits of sexiness, her cheeks flushed pink, her gaze skittering away.

He skittered, too, backpedaling from the room. And from memories not worth a damn.

So she hadn't taken off, after all, when he'd searched the house for her. Not then, at any rate. Not till later.

Didn't matter. The thought that she'd left him had been enough. Had reinforced his beliefs. Had convinced him he'd been right to hold back.

Because she'd wound up leaving, anyhow.

He could remember every word she'd spoken those last two times they'd been together, first in the ranch-house kitchen, then later in this very hall. He'd frozen into place looking at her, not believing she would really go.

He scoffed. *Never trust a woman.* He'd learned that the hard way.

Still, he'd made his offer. And she'd refused.

He thought again of how she'd walked out on him.

No way in hell would he have begged her to stay. No way would he have told her he loved her.

And he did love her, more than he'd ever believed possible.

Only, he'd wanted her to be different from the people who'd left him before. He'd wanted her to stay on the ranch forever. To love him even longer than that.

Slowly, he moved down the hall again, letting his feet lead the way without his mind thinking about it, like when he'd had to let Sunrise bring him home.

Upstairs, he passed the open door of his bedroom without stopping, not wanting to see Marissa in there.

Instead, he came to a halt, finally, in his son's bedroom.

Everything looked neat and shiny new, from the paint on the walls to the ribbons tying the bumpers against the rails.

He touched the crib, imagined his son sleeping there.

Then he waited, watched, held his breath and said a silent prayer that came from deep inside him.

Again, whatever he hoped and prayed for never happened.

Like Santa, Marissa didn't show.

ICY RAIN SLASHED the bookstore window.

Marissa set aside the inventory list Sarah had given her to check. She'd needed something to occupy her mind and hands.

Nothing could fill her heart.

She looked out through the streaked pane, feeling as miserable as the stormy weather.

Just two days had passed since she had driven away from the ranch. Away from Gabe. Already it felt like a lifetime.

She'd done the right thing, for her and the baby. She knew it.

So why did it feel so wrong?

The phone call to Father yesterday, to tell him about her pregnancy, had only made things worse.

"And this child? Boy? Or girl?"

"It's a boy, Father."

"And you're now planning to stay in Texas?"

"I don't know yet. We're trying to work things out."

"Work things out," he repeated, spacing the words. "This cowboy." He said it as he would have said "cockroach." "Is he prepared to take care of the child?"

"I have to go now, Father." Tears came to her eyes and in spite of her determination to keep her voice as cold and clipped as he did, her words were shaky. "I'll keep in touch. Goodbye."

As he had started to speak, she hung up.

She cringed now, thinking of her failure to stand up to him as she should have.

As she would have, if her own words hadn't tripped her up.

But he'd demanded answers she didn't have.

Worse, the lack of emotion in his tone had almost brought her to tears again, as she realized how much alike he and Gabe were, how similar the situations had become.

All her life, she had wanted love and emotional support, something neither of them could offer her.

The fancy schooling Father had provided, the little bit of courting Gabe had done, the financial security she'd gotten from them both—that wasn't important.

Only the emotional connection counted.

Especially with Gabe. All along, she had hated herself for not being able to separate her physical attraction to him from the emotional bonding she craved. And, all along, she should have worked at blending them together. It was the combination that would bring two people together in a happy marriage.

She knew that now. But how, with her upbringing, could she have known it before?

It was too late for any kind of relationship with Father.

And too late to mend her marriage to Gabe.

The bell over The Book Cellar's front door jingled, signaling a customer. Marissa picked up Sarah's list again, grateful for anything that would take her from her thoughts.

"Marissa?" Sarah stood in the doorway. "You've got a visitor."

Marissa's heart leaped.

Gabe.

She could barely believe it. After everything he wouldn't do, everything he refused to say, he had come to her.

But Sarah shook her head. "It's not him."

"Oh." She linked her fingers across her stomach, trying to hold back the hurt. Then she gave Sarah a smile. Small and crooked, maybe, but a genuine smile. "Only forty-eight hours in your company, and already you can read my mind. Why can't men catch on as quickly? Or, at least, one particular man?"

"If we knew that," Sarah said, "we could save the world."

Bitterness and mirth mixed in Marissa's laugh. "That's probably true. Is it Doc again?" Doc had visited her the evening before, as full of kindness and concern as always. But he'd have office hours now. "Or Mrs. Gannett?"

"He says he's your father."

She gasped. "Father? That's impossible."

"Tall and thin. White hair. And—nothing personal—but a voice that could chill a side of beef."

Stunned, Marissa nodded. "That sounds right."

"You want me to send him back here?"

"Yes, please."

A moment later, he walked into the room.

She swallowed hard. "What brings you to Dillon, Father?"

"Our conversation yesterday was not productive."

"In what way?"

"Have you found out yet whether that…cowboy is prepared to take care of the child?"

"That cowboy is my husband, and his name is Gabe Miller."

Her words triggered a memory, this time of another phone conversation. Of Gabe taking the receiver from her and announcing that he was her husband—and that he was hanging up on Father.

"Gabe and I haven't come to any agreement yet."

"That's not acceptable."

"Excuse me?" she asked, astonished by his statement.

And all too aware of his icy tone. It matched her own when she felt most frustrated with Gabe. She winced. She was more her father's daughter than she had realized.

"Obviously, the man isn't willing to take care of the child. I am."

"You?"

"He will be my heir."

"That's not enough."

"Of course not. I haven't outlined my plans. You will come back with me to New York. You will have use of the Fifth Avenue penthouse and live-in child care. Should you wish to return to work, you will have your choice of the Manhattan hotels."

She shook her head.

"Be reasonable, Marissa. It's a win-win situation."

She wanted to cry at the coldness of his offer.

As cold as the one Gabe had made to her, to live with him but keep their lives apart.

"No, Father, it's not a good situation for any of us. And my baby isn't a business deal." She took a deep, steadying breath. "What will you give him?"

"What I gave you from the time you came to live under my roof. That roof over your head, an opportunity for the best schooling, gainful employment. Everything that matters."

Marissa studied her hands.

How did she have such luck, that the two men closest to her cared nothing about what *really* mattered?

She was looking for love, something neither of them

was capable of giving. And, in that way, Father had been right. She was acting like her mother, after all, though not in the way he had meant.

They were both looking for love. But while her mother went from man to man, Marissa wanted a lifetime love. And now, she knew she deserved it. Unlike her mother, she would have the real thing someday.

That's why, though she loved Gabe, she couldn't stay with him.

Because he couldn't love her.

That's why she couldn't accept what Father had offered.

She looked up at him again. "What you want to give the baby, that list of material things. That's not enough."

"I see you've learned some negotiating skills. What else do you want?"

"For me? Nothing. For my baby?" She raised her chin and looked him in the eye. "Love. Understanding. Compassion. A grandfather who will feed him. Bathe him. Read to him before bedtime."

The expression on his face nearly made her laugh.

"Is that what you consider most important?" His scathing tone chilled her. "Use your head, Marissa. What about that child's welfare? How will you support it, with no home to speak of, no ready employment, and therefore no income?"

Several weeks ago, on her way out West, things had all seemed so much less complicated than they did right now. Several weeks ago, she hadn't been so far along in her pregnancy. Or so close to facing her future.

She folded her hands over her stomach, bowed her head and gave a deep, shuddering sigh. Now, she couldn't think about what she had done wrong in her past, what she'd missed growing up, what she wanted and needed and wished for herself.

Now, she could think only of one thing.

What was best for her baby.

COLD RAIN SOAKED Gabe's jacket, dripped off the brim of his Stetson. Fast-dropping temperatures turned his fingers numb, even inside his lined leather gloves.

Texas weather could change in a hurry, and the minor winter storm prediction had escalated into cause for major alarm. Swollen clouds scudded overhead, shoved by the fierce wind. A bolt of lightning split the dark sky.

He set to work with pliers and wire, mending the broken fence post in front of him. He didn't mind doing this job himself. Tedious work in a freezing rainstorm had suited his temperament for the past couple days. He'd been unfit to live with since his last conversations with Marissa.

Finished with his task, he shook the fence post to test its strength, then gave it a swift kick out of his own frustration.

Back in his pickup, he gunned the engine. Its powerful roar made a puny echo of the emotion raging inside him.

Not far along, he came to a stand of pines giving shelter to a few head of cattle. A half-grown calf, born just this past spring, stood close to its mother. Couldn't miss the pair, with its matched set of spotted forelegs.

A blast of icy rain hit the pickup. For a minute, Gabe couldn't see a foot in front of his face. Then the windshield cleared again.

Mama stood cuddling closer to her calf.

He thought of Marissa and how she would care for their baby. How she would shelter and cuddle their child.

He looked again at mama and calf, saw nature taking care of its own. Nature always knew best about things. Even when to let go. Sometimes, mamas rejected their babies, as his own mama had rejected him.

Just as he'd rejected Marissa and their son.

The thought sucked the wind from his lungs and stilled the beat of his heart. He was gut-punched by how badly he'd screwed up.

And how close he was coming to losing her.

All because he'd fought to be tough enough to live with her and not lose his heart. All because he'd been afraid *she* would reject *him*.

And what had she done, really, except try to love him, without knowing why he couldn't trust her, why he couldn't love her in return?

For the first time, he saw clearly what he could have, if only he'd take the chance. His wife. His son. His family.

Something he'd never wanted before, because he couldn't chance wishing for something that would never be his.

He gripped the steering wheel, fighting to steady his hands and struggling to hold back a groan.

Now, the joy of keeping Marissa and his child mattered a far sight more than his fear of rejection. Now, instead of being too afraid to trust, he was more afraid of losing everything. And so, he'd have to risk it all.

He'd have to risk his heart.

He threw the pickup into gear and floored it.

He had to get to Marissa.

It didn't matter now who knew his marriage was a sham, so long as he had the chance to make it real. To fix it. To save it.

Less than a mile later, he caught some movement out of the corner of his eye. A horse—and its rider waving to get his attention.

None of his boys would drive a horse that hard, not in this weather. Not unless they'd had an emergency. He looked at the phone cradle on the dashboard. Damn, he'd forgotten the cell.

The lone horse and rider approached. It was Warren, on Ranger. Gabe braked to a halt and jumped out of the pickup into the cold rain.

"What the hell? You oughtn't be out here in this weather—"

"Gabe," Warren broke in, gasping his name. "It's Marissa."

His blood ran cold. "What?"

"Her daddy. Came to town. Taking her home." Warren gulped a deep breath.

Gabe felt all his own breath leave his body again.

"C'mon," he said gruffly, "let's get you out of the wet."

Warren dismounted, hitched Ranger to a post beside the road and climbed into the pickup with Gabe, who flipped a switch to blast the heat.

"Thanks, boss," the older hand said, sounding more steady now. "Marissa's daddy pulled up in this fancy limousine. Wants to lure her away. Offered her a big ol' house, live-in help for the baby, and a new job in New York City."

"How do you know?"

"Sarah Jones to Doc to me."

Gabe nodded. He'd always hated the Dillon grapevine, the way news spread through town faster than a fire through drought-dry sagebrush. It'd worked like that when his mama left. And later, when the woman he was supposed to marry hightailed it out of town.

And yet again, when the woman he *had* married took off the first time. Now, she was gone once more.

Now, it was so much worse.

What could he offer Marissa that would top what her father could give her? Nothing.

Yeah, the Dillon grapevine never failed.

But *he* damn well had.

And nature had played one hell of a trick on him.

He'd finally admitted how much he felt for Marissa. He wanted her. Loved her. Needed her.

But he wouldn't get the chance to let her know.

HEEDLESS OF the wet roadway, Gabe floored the pickup, leaving Warren and Ranger as a speck in his rearview mirror, mashing the gas pedal as if his life depended on it. And it did. If only he could get to town in time. If he could just get to Marissa.

She had to come back to him. To stay with him. He'd do whatever it took. Beg, if need be—and be glad for the chance.

He took the final curve into town in a mudslinging skid, coasted onto Main Street, and almost stood on the brake in confusion. Where the hell was he headed, anyway?

Up ahead outside Sarah's bookstore, he saw his answer. A fancy-ass stretch limousine, gleaming black in the rain. Heading away from him.

He punched the gas again. Drew up alongside, then gained enough ground to slide in front of the other vehicle and slam on the brake. Tires sucked mud as the driver jerked to a stop.

He jumped out of the pickup and yanked open the limo's rear door.

A white-haired man in a megabucks suit glared at him. "What is the meaning of this?" Cold as the door handle in Gabe's hand. Icy as the sleet sliding inside his collar.

"Where's my wife?"

"I'll thank you to close the door."

Not seeing her in the car, Gabe looked around wildly, spotted Marissa hovering near the entrance to The Book Cellar, under the protective overhang.

He walked away, leaving the limo's door gaping.

Focusing only on Marissa.

As he neared, he saw the suitcase on the ground at her feet. His heart dropped to his boots, but he kept going.

He walked down the stairs and stopped beside her. The door of the bookstore stood halfway open. Just inside sat a neat pile of her suitcases. He nodded toward them and had to force words from his tight throat. "So, you're moving on."

She nodded, focused past him, out at the muddy street. "I'm leaving Sarah's, yes. To go home."

"For good?"

"I've done enough talking, Gabe. I think it's your turn."

He reached up to shift his Stetson and, to his surprise, found wet hair instead. He ran his hand through it. "Talking's not my strong suit. Guess you figured that out."

She didn't answer.

Giving him his own, back again. Well, hell, he deserved it. He gestured to the door. "If it'll keep you here, I'll talk a blue streak. But I don't want you turning blue, meanwhile."

He grabbed her suitcase and followed her into the bookstore. When he shoved the door closed, the bell jangled overhead, startling them both.

She'd sounded about as tightly strung as he felt. He found promise in that.

But her mouth settled in a straight line. Her hands, fingers twined, rested across her belly. And her eyes refused to meet his. "You had something to say?"

He nodded and took a deep breath. If ever in his life he meant to speak something worthwhile, now was the time. He hoped to hell he had what he needed inside him.

"That trip to Vegas—best thing I ever did. And you're the best thing that's ever happened to me." The need to convince her loosened his tongue, drove him on. "We're good together, Marissa. Always have been, from the minute we met. And I'm not meaning just in bed. We had good times that week in Vegas, before everything went wrong. We've had good times since. Christmas Eve. Just you and me in front of the tree, together. I want nights like that one again."

He thought of all she meant to him. Of how empty his life would be—how lost *he* would be—without her.

"I want you to come back."

He shrugged, shook his head. "Sweetheart, I couldn't compete with what your father's offering, even if I tried. All I can give you is a home. Forever. On my ranch. And in my heart."

That heart battered his ribs now as he waited. And waited. As she stood, not moving, saying nothing. He felt a rib crack. It had to have, to cause the sudden pain that pierced his chest.

Still, she kept her eyes turned away. But, at last, from under her lashes, he saw the shine of tears.

Finally, she spoke. "This is a sudden change, isn't it?"

"No, it's not. The words took a long time coming, but they were always there. I was wrong, Marissa. Way down inside, the problem didn't come from me not trusting you to stay. It came from not trusting myself to let somebody else in here." He touched his chest. "I did, right after I met you. But I was just too slab-headed to admit it to you. Or to myself."

He sighed. "I shouldn't have held you up against anyone else. You're not the same. Never were. I'm sorry for doing that. And for all the times I came to town, checking up on you. You were right about that, too. Another thing I couldn't admit."

He tilted his head, willing her to look up. Needing her to meet his eyes. If she didn't—wouldn't—he'd drop right there on the spot.

But she did, and the wave of relief almost knocked him out, anyway.

"I think we both have things to feel sorry for, Gabe. I guess I can be…slab-headed, too." One corner of her mouth curved the slightest bit. It was the most beautiful smile he'd ever seen. "It's hard to forget the past, and even harder to forgive. Maybe, sometimes, it's best to let go."

He nodded. "Yeah. I know. I'd about come to the same conclusion. Let go of the past. Concentrate on the future."

"I wasn't sure we could have a future. I thought what we had between us was lust. Sex and sparks."

"We did. We do."

She glared at him. But the lopsided smile returned. "Yes, we do. Yet we have so much more. All along, I was trying to keep a physical relationship separate from an emotional one, when really they belong together."

"That why you asked me to court you?"

"Partly. But mostly because I wanted it." She shrugged. "I wanted to feel like my life was normal, for once."

"What's normal?"

She laughed. "You know, when it comes right down

to it, I'm not sure. Neither of us has much experience in normal, do we? At least, as far as being a family." She touched her belly. "As you pointed out once, we never had the benefit of being raised with both parents."

"Yeah. And I grew up in a house full of men, till I hired Joe and Mary."

"Neither of us knows how to be a good parent."

"Does anybody, till they do it? Then doesn't it become something natural, successes and failures and all?"

"Maybe I was too afraid of the failures. You were right, in the past, about my running away. There were things I couldn't face, either. Mostly, the fact that I was too much like my mother."

"Don't let your daddy brainwash you—"

She shook her head. "No. It wasn't just him. It was me. I was afraid I was too much like her, and not even capable of loving someone." Tears sparkled in her eyes. "Looking at Father, and thinking of my mother, I know where that idea came from. But now I can see how different I am. How different you are, too. Father's cold inside, Gabe. My mother's just empty. I'm not either of those things. And neither are you."

"Hell, no, sweetheart. Not when it comes to each other. And our baby." He reached out to cover her hand, still resting on her belly. He held her gaze, feeling right. Feeling ready. "I love you, Marissa."

The half smile tugged at her lips again.

"I know," she whispered, her voice breaking. "I love you, too. I always have."

He had to shut his eyes, had to brace himself against

the rush of thankfulness overwhelming him. She loved him, always. In spite of all he hadn't done.

It was more than he deserved.

When he opened his eyes again and looked into hers, he saw a tear hanging on her bottom lash. She blinked it away.

"You were right again today, too, Gabe." Her voice caught on a sob. "I am moving on. But, this time, I'm going back to the ranch to stay, because I know that's where my home is. With you."

He swallowed hard, dropped his hands to his sides and pressed them tight. "I want to do this the right way, Marissa. And it isn't about lust or sparks or sex. It's about being honest with you. Now, and forever."

"I like that," she said.

"Can't promise I'll always remember to say pretty words, or to bring you nice things."

"That's not what I need, not what I want." She took a deep breath and stared straight into his eyes. Straight into his soul. "Can you promise to love me?"

"Done."

"Do you believe that I'll stay?"

He smiled. "That's what it all comes down to, isn't it? The loving. And the trusting."

"Yes," she said. Just that.

He drank in the sight of her for a long, long time.

She stood waiting, looking up at him, her hazel eyes dark with emotion but steady and clear.

She was there for him now. Always would be. He knew that.

He reached for her, cradled her hips with his hands. Brushed his thumbs against the sides of her belly. Brought the three of them together, the way they belonged.

"I believe in us, sweetheart," he said from his heart. "And you can trust me on that."

Epilogue

One month later

Down the other end of the diner, the heavy glass door swung closed behind Gabe.

"Did y'ever hear the likes of that?" Doc shook his head and slapped his hand on the tabletop.

Across from him, Lily Gannett's smile blazed.

Two seconds later, Delia set down the coffeepot and slipped into the chair Gabe had left. "Well?"

"Delia! Gabe just came back from Dallas—he bought Marissa an engagement ring! He said he's going to do things right from now on."

Delia gave a thumbs-up and grinned. "About time for it."

Doc snorted. "When you water the grapevine, Lily, get the details straight. What he *said* was, 'I'm plannin' to court her good and proper this time.'" He smiled, proud as if Gabe had been his own son.

He pushed his mug toward Delia. "Fill 'er up, Delia. We've got something to celebrate."

They did, right enough.

Because, considering the way he had once dragged his heels about courting his own wife, Gabe Miller had surely come around.

Three-and-a-half months after that

GABE CLOSED the kitchen door behind him and hung his Stetson on the peg beside the door.

Marissa had turned off the kitchen light, left the one over the sink burning. Meaning she'd headed up to bed already.

He set his boots in one corner and walked out of the room in his socks. She was a light sleeper, he'd come to find out. He chuckled, thinking of those times she'd played possum New Year's week, pretending to be asleep when he'd come into the bedroom.

No need for that now—though, more often than not lately, she fell asleep shortly after they hit the hay. Fine by him. She'd been awfully tired the past few weeks, with the baby due any day.

He reached for the hallway light, flicked it on.

And found Marissa standing at the top of the stairway, holding a suitcase.

They'd renewed their vows a few months back, in a proper church ceremony. He ran his thumb across the gold ring on his left hand, third finger. Thought of what she'd had inscribed inside.

Forever, M

He stared up at her.

"I'm sorry, Gabe," she said, "but I have to leave."

Once, she'd stood there and said that, and his heart had almost broken.

Now, it swelled with joy.

He ran up the steps and took the suitcase from her. Took her by the arm. "It's time?"

She smiled. "Our son wants to make his entrance."

"Let's get moving, then." He walked her carefully down the stairs and along the hall to the kitchen.

"Aren't you forgetting something?"

Once, he'd said that to her. "You want to kiss your hardworking husband?"

"Yes." She grazed his cheek with her lips. "But that's not it."

"Call Doc?"

"He'll be at the hospital."

"What, then?"

She pointed downward.

"Oh. Yeah." He grabbed his boots from the corner, nearly poured his feet into them. Grinning, he opened the kitchen door.

The pickup was right outside.

"Did I tell you you're the best wife I could ever have?"

"Only twelve times this week."

"I'll work on it."

He helped her into the front seat, wrapped the seat

belt around her. Then he stood still, just for a moment. Just long enough to give thanks for having her there.

As he knew he would, every day of his life.

When she reached out to touch his cheek, his breath lodged in his throat.

"Did I tell you I'll never leave you?" she whispered.

With his heart near ready to burst, he had to force himself to sound stern. "Couldn't prove it by tonight, now, could you?"

"Come on, cowboy." Laughing, she shook her head. "You know trips to the maternity ward don't count."

* * * * *

New York Times *bestselling author*
Linda Lael Miller
is back with a new romance
featuring the heartwarming McKettrick family
from Silhouette Special Edition.

SIERRA'S HOMECOMING
by Linda Lael Miller

On sale December 2006,
wherever books are sold.

Turn the page for a sneak preview!

Soft, smoky music poured into the room.

The next thing she knew, Sierra was in Travis's arms, close against that chest she'd admired earlier, and they were slow dancing.

Why didn't she pull away?

"Relax," he said. His breath was warm in her hair.

She giggled, more nervous than amused. What was the matter with her? She was attracted to Travis, had been from the first, and he was clearly attracted to her. They were both adults. Why not enjoy a little slow dancing in a ranch-house kitchen?

Because slow dancing led to other things. She took a step back and felt the counter flush against her lower back. Travis naturally came with her, since they were holding hands and he had one arm around her waist.

Simple physics.

Then he kissed her.

Physics again—this time, not so simple.

"Yikes," she said, when their mouths parted.

He grinned. "Nobody's ever said that after I kissed them."

She felt the heat and substance of his body pressed against hers. "It's going to happen, isn't it?" she heard herself whisper.

"Yep," Travis answered.

"But not tonight," Sierra said on a sigh.

"Probably not," Travis agreed.

"When, then?"

He chuckled, gave her a slow, nibbling kiss. "Tomorrow morning," he said. "After you drop Liam off at school."

"Isn't that…a little…soon?"

"Not soon enough," Travis answered, his voice husky. "Not nearly soon enough."

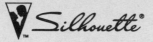

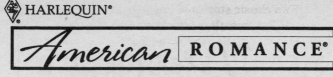

HARLEQUIN®

American ROMANCE®

IS PROUD TO PRESENT

COWBOY VET
by Pamela Britton

Jessie Monroe is the last person on earth
Rand Sheppard wants to rely on, but he needs
a veterinary technician—yesterday—and she's the
only one for hire. It turns out the woman who
destroyed his cousin's life isn't who Rand thought
she was. And now she's all he can think about!

"Pamela Britton writes the kind of
wonderfully romantic, sexy, witty romance
that readers dream of discovering
when they go into a bookstore."

—*New York Times* bestselling author
Jayne Ann Krentz

Cowboy Vet *is available from*
Harlequin American Romance in December 2006.

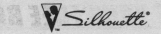

REQUEST YOUR FREE BOOKS!
2 FREE NOVELS PLUS 2
FREE GIFTS!

Heart, Home & Happiness!

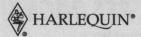

HARLEQUIN®

American ROMANCE®

COMING NEXT MONTH

#1141 A LARAMIE, TEXAS CHRISTMAS by Cathy Gillen Thacker
The McCabes: Next Generation
All Kevin McCabe wants for Christmas is to get closer to Noelle Kringle.
She and her son are in Laramie for the holidays, and he finds himself strongly
attracted to her. He can tell the feeling is mutual, but as quickly as Kevin's
falling in love, he can't help but wonder what it is she's trying to hide.

#1142 TEMPTED BY A TEXAN by Mindy Neff
Texas Sweethearts
Becca Sue Ellsworth's prospects for cuddling a child of her own seem grim,
until the night her old flame arrives first on the scene of a break-in to rescue her
from a prowler. Suddenly she realizes she has another chance to get Colby Flynn
to rethink his ambition to be a big-city lawyer—and to remind the long, tall
Texan of a baby-making promise seven years ago…the one she'd gotten from him!

#1143 COWBOY VET by Pamela Britton
Jessie Monroe is the last person on earth Rand Sheppard wants to rely on, but
he needs a veterinary technician—yesterday—and she's the only one for hire.
It turns out the woman who destroyed his cousin's life isn't who Rand thought
she was. And now she's all he can think about.…

#1144 THE WEDDING SECRET by Michele Dunaway
American Beauties
After landing a plum position on the hottest talk show in the country,
Cecile Duletsky is ready for just about anything. Anything but gorgeous
Luke Shaw, that is. Cecile spends a fabulous night with him, knowing she isn't
ready for a complicated romance. But that's before she shows up for work and
finds Luke—her boss—sitting across from her in the boardroom.

www.eHarlequin.com